The Seven-Year-Old Wonder Book

For everyone who has ever been seven years old
or is,
or soon will be

The Seven-Year-Old
Wonder Book

Isabel Wyatt

Floris Books

Illustrations by Alyson MacNeill

First published in 1958
This third edition published in 2012 by Floris Books

British Library CIP Data available
ISBN 978-086315-943-5

Printed in Poland

Contents

Sylvia and the Sick Toys

Sylvia lived with her mother in a white cottage at the edge of a dark wood. There was a nut hedge round the garden, and in this hedge was a tall tree which Sylvia loved to climb.

One stormy afternoon she was sitting on a branch high up in the tree. The wind was so strong that her branch swayed back and forth. Suddenly there was a loud crack, and Sylvia found herself falling – falling – falling – crashing through the branches below, which seemed to hold out their arms to catch her, and pass her down until the lowest branch dropped her, trembling, on the grass.

Sylvia wanted to cry; but she didn't want to hurt the tree's feelings after it had tried so hard to save her. So she thanked the tree as bravely as she could, and limped inside to see her mother.

Her mother gently washed the scratches on her knee, and rubbed on some sweet-smelling pink cream, and covered it all with a soft white bandage, till Sylvia's knee felt better than the rest of her.

Now some of Sylvia's toys had had accidents, too. Pip, her red velvet dog, had wagged his tail off; Bruno, her brown bear, had lost an eye; and Jumbo, the father elephant, had sprained his trunk. Titania, her fairy doll, had torn her wings on a bad-tempered nail; Goldilocks' eyelids were stuck wide open, so that she couldn't get to sleep; and Kate, who was quite an old baby doll, had lost so much of her sawdust stuffing she was all saggy.

So Sylvia sat them in a row, and gently washed the sick places, and rubbed on some sweet-smelling pink cream, and covered them all up with a soft white bandage, until the sick places felt better than the rest of them.

Sylvia asked her mother:

"How soon will we all be better, Mother?"

And her mother replied:

"As soon as you wake in the morning, Sylvia, if you go to the fountain of dew tonight, like the wood-maiden who couldn't dance."

Then Sylvia begged:

"Oh, Mother, please tell us about her!"

And her mother promised:

"Tonight, then, in bed."

So at bedtime, when Sylvia and Pip and Bruno and Jumbo and Titania and Goldilocks and Kate were cuddled under the blankets together, Sylvia's mother sat at the foot of the bed and told them the story of the wood-maiden who couldn't dance.

And this is it:

The Story of the Wood-Maiden
Who Couldn't Dance

There was once a little wood-maiden, who lived all alone in an ivy house in the middle of a forest. She had fallen out of a tree and hurt herself, so she could no longer run and dance with the other wood-maidens.

One black and stormy night, there was a knock at her door. She felt a little frightened; but she bravely opened the door, and there in the dark and rain stood a little old woman, all blown about and wet through.

The wood-maiden felt so sorry for her that she completely forgot about being frightened; she took her by the hand, and brought her in, and dried her clothes, and made her comfortable by the fire, and brought her some strawberries and milk.

When the little old woman had eaten the strawberries and drunk the milk, she asked:

"If you could have a wish, dear child, what would it be?"

And the wood-maiden answered:

"Oh, I'd wish to be able to run and dance again with the other wood-maidens."

Then the little old woman said:

"Because you have been brave and opened the door although you were frightened, and because you have been kind to an old woman, I will tell you how to make your wish come true. In the Land of the Singing Sky there is a fountain of dew; and if you sip one drop of it, it will make you well again."

The wood-maiden sighed with joy at the thought; and she asked:

"Where *is* the Land of the Singing Sky?"

And the little old woman replied:

"At the top of the silver ladder which hangs from the full moon."

The little wood-maiden thanked her very happily, and made a pile of fern and heather in the corner to make a bed for her. But when she turned round, the little old woman had disappeared.

As soon as there was a full moon, the wood-maiden went through the forest to the bottom of its silver ladder. And there she found a beautiful lady, who smiled at her and asked:

"What are you looking for, little wood-maiden?"

And the wood-maiden answered:

"Please, I have come to climb the silver ladder to the Land of the Singing Sky, to sip one drop of the fountain of dew, which will make me well again."

Then the beautiful lady said:

"But don't you know, little wood-maiden, that you can only do that if you bring six others with you?"

So the wood-maiden went away; and on the trunks of the big trees at the four corners of the forest she wrote that if anyone needed to be made better they should come to her ivy house before the next full moon.

But the days went by, and the nights went by, and nobody came, till at last there were only seven nights left till the moon would be full again.

That night there was a knock at the door; and when the wood-maiden opened it, outside stood a lion cub who had thorn stuck in one of his paws.

And the wood-maiden said:

"Come in, you poor lion cub, and stay with me till the moon is full; and then we can both go and sip one drop of the fountain of dew together."

So the lion cub came in.

On the second night there was a knock at the door; and when the wood-maiden opened it, outside stood a honey bear with his nose sore where bees had stung him.

And the wood-maiden said:

"Come in, you poor honey bear, and stay with lion cub and me till the moon is full; and then all three of us can go and sip one drop of the fountain of dew together."

So the honey bear came in.

On the third night there was a knock at the door; and when the wood-maiden opened it, outside stood a little boy with his arm in a sling.

And the wood-maiden said:

"Come in, you poor little boy, and stay with honey bear and lion cub and me till the moon is full; and then all four of us can go and sip one drop of the fountain of dew together."

11

So the little boy came in.

On the fourth night there was a knock at the door; and when the wood-maiden opened it, outside stood a white swan with a dragging wing.

And the wood-maiden said:

"Come in, you poor swan, and stay with little boy and honey bear and lion cub and me till the moon is full; and then all five of us can go and sip one drop of the fountain of dew together."

So the white swan came in.

On the fifth night there was a knock at the door; and when the wood-maiden opened it, outside stood a tiny green lizard with only a stump where its long tail should have been.

And the wood-maiden said:

"Come in, you poor lizard, and stay with swan and little boy and honey bear and lion cub and me till the moon is full; and then all six of us can go and sip one drop of the fountain of dew together."

So the tiny green lizard came in.

On the sixth night there was a knock at the door; and when the wood-maiden opened it, outside stood a dwarf with one foot all wrapped up in bandages.

And the wood-maiden said:

"Come in, you poor dwarf, and stay with lizard and swan and little boy and honey bear and lion cub and me till the moon is full; and then all seven of us can go and sip one drop of the fountain of dew together."

So the dwarf came in.

And now there were the six others with the wood-maiden in the little ivy house who needed to be made well again.

But on the seventh night, the night before full moon, there was another knock at the door; and when the wood-maiden opened it, outside stood a water nixie with a wound in her throat where a swordfish had attacked her.

The wood-maiden stood silently a moment, because the

water nixie would make one too many; but she felt so sorry for her that she couldn't send her away.

So she said to her also:

"Come in, you poor water nixie, and stay the night with dwarf and lizard and swan and little boy and honey bear and lion cub and me; and tomorrow, when the moon is full, all eight of us can go and *try* to sip one drop of the fountain of dew together."

So the water nixie came in.

The next night the moon was full, and they all went together through the forest to the bottom of its silver ladder. The beautiful lady was waiting for them. One by one she helped them climb up the silver ladder; and at the top they came to the Land of the Singing Sky.

From all around them came the sweetest singing they had ever heard. There were meadows filled with growing stars and every star was singing. And singing children were flying among the stars on rosy wings.

And as the wood-maiden looked at them, she thought:

"Oh, if only *I* could fly among the stars like that!"

The beautiful lady led them to the fountain of dew, and she said to the wood-maiden:

"Hold out your hands, little wood-maiden, and catch the rainbow-coloured spray."

So the wood-maiden cupped her hands and held them towards the fountain of dew; and seven drops of the rainbow-coloured spray fell into them.

Then the beautiful lady said:

"You may only have seven drops. But there are eight of you. Which one will go without?"

Then the wood-maiden looked round slowly at them all – at the water nixie with the swordfish wound on her throat; at the dwarf with his bandaged foot; at the tiny green lizard in need of a new tail; at the white swan with her dragging wing; at the little boy with his arm in a sling; at the honey bear with his huge, sore, swollen nose; at the lion cub with his wounded paw. She thought they all deserved a drop from the fountain of dew. So she sighed, and turned to the beautiful lady, and said: "I will be the one who doesn't take a drop."

Then she held out her cupped hands to the water nixie. And the water nixie sipped one drop; and at once the wound in her throat was well again. And the water nixie thanked her.

Then she held out her cupped hands to the dwarf. And the dwarf sipped one drop; and at once his broken foot was well again. And the dwarf thanked her.

Then she held out her cupped hands to the tiny green lizard. And the tiny green lizard sipped one drop; and at once it grew a fine new tail. And the tiny green lizard thanked her.

Then she held out her cupped hands to the white swan. And the white swan sipped one drop; and at once her dragging wing was well again. And the white swan thanked her.

Then she held out her cupped hands to the little boy. And the little boy sipped one drop; and at once his broken arm was well again. And the little boy thanked her.

Then she held out her cupped hands to the honey bear. And the honey bear sipped one drop; and at once the stings stopped hurting, and his huge, sore, swollen nose was the size a honey bear's nose ought to be again. And the honey bear thanked her.

Then she held out her cupped hands to the lion cub. And the lion cub sipped one drop; and at once the thorn came out and his paw was well again. And the lion cub thanked her.

Then she looked inside her hands but they were empty. Then the beautiful lady, standing close to the fountain of dew, called to her:

"Little wood-maiden, come and dance with me!"

And the wood-maiden answered sadly:

"I cannot dance."

But the beautiful lady asked her again:

"Come and try!"

14

So the wood-maiden came towards her, and took her hand; and the rainbow-coloured spray from the fountain of dew fell all about her, and she began to try to dance. And she found that she *could* dance; she could run and dance and leap just as well as she could before she fell out of the tree. She had been made better.

And when she finally stopped dancing, the water nixie and the dwarf and the lizard and the swan and the little boy and the honey bear and the lion cub had gone. And the full moon and its silver ladder were gone as well.

And she cried:

"Oh dear, the silver ladder's gone! How will I get down to my little ivy house?"

And the beautiful lady smiled and asked:

"Why not use your wings?"

And the wood-maiden looked over her shoulder, and she saw that she now had rosy wings just like the happy children she had watched flying over the meadows of stars.

And as she was spreading them the beautiful lady said:

"You can come every night to the fountain of dew, little wood-maiden. You do not need to wait for the full moon's silver ladder now you have found your wings."

So the wood-maiden flew happily down to her little ivy house, and folded her wings, and went inside. And in the morning she ran happily through the forest to join the other wood-maidens in their dancing once again.

The Poem of the Singing Sky

When the story was finished, Sylvia sighed and said:

"I wish I could fly among the stars and hear them singing!"

And her mother answered:

"So you do – every night!"

And Sylvia said:

"Yes, but when I wake up I forget. I wonder if the rhyme-elves would paint a poem to remind me?"

You see Sylvia had a Wonder Book, which the rhyme-elves painted poems in for her during the night. Before she went to sleep, she would put the book on her bedside table, and chant a magic spell. And the next morning, when she woke up, the book would be opened at a new page. And on the new page there would be a new poem, beautifully painted in big letters, with a picture to go with it like the pictures in this book.

So Sylvia reached under her pillow for her Wonder Book, and put it on the table. And when her mother had tucked her and all the sick toys into bed, and said goodnight, and gone quietly downstairs, Sylvia softly chanted her magic spell. And this was it:

> "Rhyme-elves, rich in ringing words
> Won from winds and waves and birds,
> Lisping leaves and rustling rain,
> Sing – sing – for me again!"

As soon as she woke up the next morning she took off her bandage, and she found that her knee was healed. Then she woke up the sick toys, and took off their bandages. And she found that Kate, the saggy baby doll, was quite plump again; and Bruno, the brown bear, had both eyes again; and Titania, the fairy doll, had new wings and could fly again; and Pip, the red velvet dog, could wag his tail again; and Goldilocks could go to sleep again; and Jumbo, the father elephant, could swing his trunk again.

So, hugging them all, and her Wonder Book, Sylvia ran into her mother's room, woke her up, and showed her all how all the toys had been healed, and asked:

"Does that mean we found the fountain of dew last night, Mother, like the wood-maiden who couldn't dance?"

And her mother smiled, and answered:

"Of course you did!"

Then Kate and Bruno and Titania and Pip and Goldilocks and Jumbo and Sylvia all scrambled into Sylvia's mother's bed; and Sylvia opened her Wonder Book at the new page, and together they all looked happily at its two new pictures – a big coloured one of the wood-maiden meeting the beautiful lady, and a small one of the wood-maiden, dancing happily into her little ivy house.

And then Sylvia's mother read them the new poem. And this is what she read:

> At night in bed I feel the windy beat
> Of rosy wings.
> The sky is filled with music soft and sweet,
> Which each star sings.
> Bright fields of singing stars go drifting by;
> And in them happy children sing and fly;
> And with them – I.
> I do not hear the singing stars by day,
> Nor spread my wings.
> I am too brisk and busy with my play
> And waking things.
> But music breathes again as night draws nigh,
> Till flocks of children throng the singing sky,
> And with them – I.

Sister-in-the-Bushes

As soon as Sylvia got dressed, she ran through the garden to her tall tree, and put her hands on the trunk and whispered:

"I found the fountain of dew last night, so my knee's much, much better, thank you."

And, just to show the tree how well her knee was, she began to climb it again.

She was just about to reach the branch that she'd fallen from yesterday, when a soft voice murmured in her ear:

"Not that branch, Sylvia!"

And when Sylvia turned, she saw, just behind and above her, among the green leaves, there stood a little girl. She was dressed all in white and her golden hair was so bright that it made Sylvia think of the flame of a candle.

Sylvia stared and stared; and at last she gasped:

"Oh, aren't you lovely! Please tell me who you are."

And the shining child replied:

"I am your sister."

Then Sylvia said:

"But you don't live with us."

And the shining child replied:

"No; I am your Sister-in-the-Bushes."

Then Sylvia asked:

"Won't you come and live with us in our white cottage? I've got a lovely mother."

And the shining child replied:

"I know – I have watched you together. But I don't want to live inside a house. I like living in the bushes."

Sylvia tried to persuade the girl to come with her:

"But if you came, then we could play together."

And the shining child replied:

"We can do that anyway. Whenever you want me, just go to the bushes and call me, and I'll come."

Sylvia was so excited about this that she clapped her hands; and then she asked:

"Sister-in-the-Bushes, how long have you lived in the bushes?"

And Sister-in-the-Bushes answered:

"As long as you have lived inside a house."

Then Sylvia asked again:

"Then why have I never seen you before?"

And Sister-in-the-Bushes answered:

"Perhaps because I'm shy. But today I forgot to be shy because you were in danger. Come and look!"

So Sylvia climbed up beside her, and from there she could see that the branch that she'd fallen from yesterday was broken, and that if she had climbed onto it she would have fallen again. So she thanked Sister-in-the-Bushes for saving her today, and the tall tree all over again for saving her yesterday; and just then her mother called from the cottage door that breakfast was ready.

And as Sylvia ate her porridge and drank her milk she was so happy she couldn't keep still. She told her mother all about Sister-in-the-Bushes and begged:

"Please can I play with her, Mother?"

And her mother answered, smiling:

"Of course you may."

Then Sylvia asked:

"Mother, did you have a Sister-in-the-Bushes, too?"

And her mother replied:

"Everyone has a Sister-in-the-Bushes, but sometimes they

never find her. But she is always there, watching over them, like Princess Helia with Princess Merry."

And Sylvia cried:

"Oh, Mother, will you tell me about them?"

And her mother promised:

"When bedtime comes."

When it was bedtime, Sylvia chose Titania, her fairy doll, to take to bed with her, because, although her Sister-in-the-Bushes didn't have wings or a magic wand with a star at the top, like Titania, they reminded her a little of each other.

And this is the story of the star twins, which her mother told Sylvia and Titania when she had tucked them into bed:

The Story of the Star Twins

The Queen of the Stars was named Urania. She had many children and all of them were born with a star on their foreheads. All of her children had already grown up and left her palace to rule a star of their own, except her two youngest daughters. They were twins called Princess Merry and Princess Helia. Merry was a strong, noisy, boisterous little princess, while Helia was pale and quiet; but they loved each other very much and didn't want to be apart for a minute.

One day the boisterous Princess Merry said to the quiet Princess Helia:

"Helia, come with me to the Black Country!"

The gentle Princess Helia shivered:

"Oh, Merry, please don't go to that terrible land!"

And Merry answered:

"But, Helia, I want to free the poor people who live there from the greedy witch."

So the two star princesses went to their mother and told her about Merry's plan. And Queen Urania said:

"I'm very proud of you Merry for wanting to go to the Black Country, to try to free the greedy witch's slaves. But Helia is too delicate to go to such a horrible place. I'm afraid my dear daughters, that it's time for you to split up."

The twin princesses were sad at the thought of parting. But Merry was desperate to free the witch's slaves and she knew that she had to go. So one day she said goodbye to her mother and her gentle sister Helia and set out on her journey. She wore a dress made out of starlight, kept her star upon her forehead and took with her two coins of starry gold.

When she came to the shore of the Sea of the Nether Sky, she found a ship and asked the captain to take her across the sea to the Black Country. She paid him with one of her two coins of starry gold.

At midnight, when the ship was still at sea, a storm blew up which was so fierce that the captain worried the ship would sink. But Princess Merry stood at the front of the ship through the worst part of the storm; and with the star on her forehead shining and wearing her dress made out of starlight, she guided the ship safely to the shore of the Black Country.

The Black Country was a bleak and gloomy land. The greedy witch made all the people her slaves and forced them to go down into the mines to get precious stones for her. In the Cavern of Gloom, where she lived, she had tens of thousands and hundreds of thousands and thousands of thousands of jewels. But she was never satisfied. The more jewels her poor slaves found for her, the more she made them find.

Merry began her journey across the Black Country and saw many of the greedy witch's slaves. She felt sorry for the poor people in their coal-black cloaks and miserable expressions. In return the greedy witch's slaves couldn't stop staring at this shining princess in her dress made out of starlight and with a star on her forehead.

Some of them stared at her in joy and wonder; but some of them tried to snatch away the star and the gleaming dress. So with her second coin of starry gold Merry bought a black cloak and hood, like everyone else in the Black Country wore. She tightly wrapped the cloak over her dress of starlight, and she pulled down the hood over the star on her forehead, so that no one who met her would ever guess how beautiful she was inside.

So she travelled safely through the Black Country until at last she came to the Cavern of Gloom. As she felt her way inside, it grew darker and darker, till suddenly she turned a corner, and there before her sat the greedy witch. The witch was gloating over the enormous heaps of jewels which shone and flashed and sparkled and lit up the shadowy cave.

Now before Princess Merry had left her mother's palace, Queen Urania had taught her a magic word which would control the greedy witch. But she'd wrapped her black cloak and hood so tightly around her that she'd forgotten it. So when the greedy witch looked up and saw the star princess standing in front of her, it was she who spoke first. Quickly she said a spell which turned Merry into a small black spider.

And she drove the spider into a corner of the cave, yelling:

"Spin – spin – spin!
Grey miles of gossamer
To wrap my jewels in.
Do not move from this corner.
Spin – spin – spin!"

Now in Queen Urania's palace among the stars there was a wonderful picture gallery. On its walls, framed in gold, hung portraits of all the star princesses and star princes who were her children. When they were well and happy, their portraits smiled and sang; but if they were unhappy or in danger, their portraits wept.

Princess Helia was always thinking about her twin sister Merry so three times a day she visited Merry's portrait to make sure that she was alright. And at first the portrait smiled and sang; but one day she found it weeping.

Helia ran to Queen Urania, crying:

"Oh, Mother, something terrible has happened to Merry! I have to help her!"

And Queen Urania said:

"But, Helia, it would kill you to go to the Black Country!"

But Helia insisted:

"Not if I go to help Merry."

Then Queen Urania quickly to look at Merry's portrait; and as soon as she saw it weeping, she said:

"The greedy witch has laid a spell upon her. Yes, Helia, you must go. You are the only one who can set her free. But if you put on a black cloak and hood, you will lose yourself and your memories just like she did. So instead I will give you a cloak and hood of dark blue air to cover your dress of starlight and the star on your forehead."

Then she took Queen Urania taught Helia the magic word which she could use to the greedy witch, and a second magic word which would reverse the spell which Merry was under. Helia said goodbye to her mother, and set out on her journey, taking with her the cloak and hood of dark blue air and one coin of starry gold.

When she came to the shore of the Sea of the Nether Sky, she found a ship; but she was too shy to ask the captain to take her to the Black Country. Instead she laid her coin of starry gold on the deck, and floated up among the sails, wrapped in her cloak and hood of dark blue air.

At midnight, when the ship was still at sea, a storm blew up which was so fierce that the captain worried the ship would sink.

23

Helia took off her cloak and hood and stood at the top of the mast through the worst part of the storm. With the star shining on her forehead and her dress made out of starlight, she guided the ship safely to the shore of the Black Country.

There Helia wrapped herself again in her cloak and hood and swiftly, but safely, travelled to the Cavern of Gloom. As she felt her way inside, it grew darker and darker, till suddenly she turned a corner, and there before her sat the greedy witch. The witch was wrapping her enormous heaps of jewels in miles and miles of grey gossamer.

Then Helia threw off her cloak and hood and the star on her forehead blazed brightly and her dress of starlight gleamed and glittered. She was so bright that she outshone the light coming from of all the witch's jewels.

The witch looked up in alarm but before she could say her spell, Helia loudly said the magic word that would control her. When the witch heard the magic word she fell on her knees, and trembled, and cried for mercy.

Then Helia demanded:

"Where is the star princess that you put a spell on?"

The kneeling witch pointed humbly to the corner of her cave where a small black spider was spinning miles and miles of grey gossamer.

Helia went to the corner and gently spoke the second magic word. As soon as she heard it the small black spider turned back into a star princess, and the two sisters hugged each other tightly.

The twin star princesses set free all the slaves in the Black Country and made sure that each of them had their fair share of the jewels in the Cavern of Gloom. Defeated, the greedy witch begged:

"Please take me back with you across the Sea of the Nether Sky, so that the Queen of the Stars can teach me how to become good."

24

So they took the witch home with them to Queen Urania's palace. When the Queen heard their story, she said:

"You never need to be apart again, my dear daughters, for I will give you twin stars to rule. And because you led the ships safely to shore, your twin stars shall do the same."

So the boisterous Princess Merry and the gentle Princess Helia were never split up again; and we can look up at the sky and see the stars they rule. And we call their stars the Heavenly Twins.

The Poem of the Black Cloak and Hood

Before Sylvia went to sleep, her mother held back the curtain and showed her the twin stars shining in the sky. Then Sylvia put out her Wonder Book on the bedside table, and softly chanted her poetry spell:

"Rhyme-elves, rich in ringing words
Won from winds and waves and birds,
Lisping leaves and rustling rain,
Sing – sing – for me again!"

When she woke up the next morning, the curtains were still closed; and in the half-dark she could see a star shining on the pillow beside her. She jumped out of bed and climbed on the window seat drawing the curtains back so she could see better. The star on her pillow was the one from Titania's magic wand. Titania must have moved a little in her sleep, so that it shone now on her forehead. Sylvia stared at herself in the mirror, and thought:

"There's a star on my forehead, too, only my black hood covers it."

Then she turned to her open Wonder Book; and she saw that there was a new poem, with a picture of Princess Merry guiding the ship through the storm. So she and Titania took the Wonder Book into her mother's bed. After they had showed her the picture, her mother read the new poem to them:

When down to the dark Earth I sped
From where the stately stars are spread,
I set a black hood on my head.
But under it I still wear now
A secret star upon my brow.

In Earth's chill winds to keep me warm,
I wrapped a black cloak round my form.
But under it, where none can see,
My starlight dress still gleams on me.

Some day, shedding my dark disguise,
I shall shine starry as the skies,
And with my heavenly twin shall fare
Back to the home we used to share,
To rule twin stars together there.

The Making of the Fairy Tree

Sylvia was in the garden, helping her mother to gather the ripe seeds, when suddenly she stopped to ask:

"Mother, how can a big plant come out of this tiny seed?"

Sylvia's mother straightened her back and said, smiling:

"That's something your Sister-in-the-Bushes might show you!"

So Sylvia went to the bushes, and called out:

"Please, Sister-in-the-Bushes, could you show me how a big plant comes out of this tiny seed?"

Then Sister-in-the-Bushes came out from among the leaves with a blue flower in her hand. And she answered:

"I'll try, Sylvia. Close your eyes!"

Sylvia closed her eyes and Sister-in-the-Bushes touched them with the blue flower. When she opened them the ground had become as clear as glass so that she could see deep down into it. The stems of the plants had become fountains of green water, the leaves seemed to be made of green light, and coloured flames were leaping from the flowers. All around her the air was filled with floating rainbows and tiny flashes of multi-coloured lights played round the bees and the butterflies.

Then Sister-in-the-Bushes called quietly:

"Earth fairies, can Sylvia see you make a fairy tree?"

And out of the clear ground at Sylvia's feet came hurrying

tiny knights in shining armour. They looked around, staring right through Sylvia; and their leader asked:

"But where is Sylvia? Oh dear, is she not seven yet?"

And Sylvia said:

"Not till New Year's Eve."

And he nodded his head, and said:

"We can't see little children till they're seven. But give me your seed, Sylvia. We can still show you how a fairy tree is made."

So Sylvia bent down and gave him her seed, which he laid on the ground. Then all the tiny knights sank into the clear earth again, and lifted their hands, and called together:

"Sink down to us, little seed!"

As the seed sank slowly down into the earth towards them a green fairy fire began to burn all round it and a white root tip appeared. The little knights sank deeper still, and lifted their hands, and called together:

"Grow down to us, little root!"

The white root stretched out, down towards them. They scooped up handfuls of milk from the clear earth and gave it to the root to drink.

As the root drank, a shoot peeped out from the top of the seed. The tiny knights rose and gathered above it, and called together:

"Grow up to us, little shoot!"

The shoot grew up through the clear earth and came out into the light. On the surface of the ground it spread two leaves and between them grew a straight green stalk.

Then Sister-in-the-Bushes again called softly:

"Dew fairies, can Sylvia see you make a fairy tree?"

Then the tiny mermaids who had been swimming in the dewdrops came gathering round the green stalk, and swam in and out about it, murmuring together:

"Grow upwards, little stalk, into the sunshine! Come out from the stalk, little leaves!"

The stalk grew taller, and its leaves began to grow.

The mermaids brought dewdrops and the leaves drank them.

Then Sister-in-the-Bushes again called softly:

"Air fairies, can Sylvia see you make a fairy tree?"

Then the winged fairies who had been following the birds came flying down, and the air all round them was like misty fire. And with this they fed the leaves, singing together:

"Grow, fairy tree! Come out, little bud!"

The plant went on growing until a flower bud appeared.

Then Sister-in-the-Bushes again called softly:

"Fire fairies, can Sylvia see you make a fairy tree?"

Then the fairies, who looked like flames and were riding the bees and the butterflies, flew to the fairy tree and danced around the flower bud, whispering together:

"Open, flower, and ripen, fruit!"

Surrounded by their warmth the flower opened, curled back its petals and let the warmed pollen grains fall into the warmed seed box. With the help of the fairy warmth the seed box grew into a ripe fruit, which split to show the seeds inside, ready to be scattered. Sister-in-the-Bushes took one of the seeds and gave it back to Sylvia.

Sylvia thanked all the fairies, and Sister-in-the-Bushes too, and ran back to her mother. She told her all about how the knights and the fairies had made her seed grow and showed her mother the fairies' seed. Then she carefully planted it in a very special place in her own little garden, with a ring of white pebbles round it to mark the exact spot. And she felt as happy as if she had been given a very special gift.

And indeed, a special gift was exactly what she'd been given.

The Poem of the Tree Makers

Sylvia took Titania to bed again with her that night because she was a fairy like those who had helped her seed grow in the garden. As her mother tucked them in, Sylvia said:

"Mother, we haven't had a story today, so what will the rhyme-elves paint my poem about?"

And her mother asked her:

"What would you like it to be about, if you could choose?"

Sylvia said at once:

"Oh, I would want a poem about the making of the fairy tree because that was the best thing that happened to me today."

Her mother replied:

"Then I expect that's what their poem will be about, Sylvia, because they like making poems about lovely things that happen as well as about stories."

So Sylvia put out her Wonder Book, open at a new page, and quietly chanted her poetry spell:

> "Rhyme-elves, rich in ringing words
> Won from winds and waves and birds,
> Lisping leaves and rustling rain,
> Sing – sing – for me again!"

And when she woke up the next morning, there was a new poem on the new page of the Wonder Book. When Sylvia saw the new poem's new picture, she gave an "Oh!" of delight, because it was a portrait of herself watching the fairy tree being made. She and Titania jumped quickly out of bed and ran to show the picture to her mother. When they had all looked at it together, this was the new poem which Sylvia's mother read to them:

In leaf and stem, water;
Earth in the root;
Air in the blossom;
Fire in the fruit.
Fairies of Water,
Fire, Air and Earth
Ceaselessly toil that
A plant may have birth.

The Dragon in the Sky

In another white cottage in another part of the dark wood lived Sylvia's friend, an old woodsman. He lived all alone except for Blackbird, his black pony. Whenever Blackbird came by with a load of logs for the village, she would stop at Sylvia's cottage to take Sylvia for a ride too. So when, the morning after Sylvia saw the fairy tree made, she heard *clip – clop – clop* along the woodland path, she cried eagerly:

"Mother, Blackbird's coming! Can I go for a ride with her?"

Her mother answered:

"Yes, and will you ask Mr Woodsman nicely whether we may have some more logs, please? Now that autumn has arrived we'll soon need to keep our fires burning all day long."

So Sylvia ran to the gate and waited for Blackbird. Soon she came along with the logs neatly piled in the cart behind her and with the old woodsman walking beside her. Sylvie always thought how kind he looked in his shabby corduroy trousers and his old, old hat. He took Sylvia up in his arms, swung her on to Blackbird's back, and held her safely with one of his huge strong hands. Sylvia swayed gently with Blackbird's gentle movements and listened with open ears to the old woodsman saying because there was nothing he didn't know about the woods.

Today he said, in his slow, cosy voice:

"See how the leaves are turning yellow, Sylvia! Any day now, Knight Michael's wind will start blowing them away."

Sylvia asked:

"Why is the wind Knight Michael's wind, Mr Woodsman?"

He replied:

"Because it comes from the rushing of his sword as he fights the dragon. Didn't you know that every autumn, when the leaves turn yellow, Knight Michael fights the dragon in the sky?"

Sylvia was still thinking about this when Blackbird set her down again at the gate of her white cottage. She went into the garden and found Sister-in-the-Bushes lying on the grass and staring at the wide, bright, empty sky. Sylvia asked her:

"What on earth are you staring at, Sister-in-the-Bushes?"

Sister-in-the-Bushes answered:

"Close your eyes and come and see."

She pulled Sylvia down beside her and touched her closed eyelids again with her blue flower.

When Sylvia opened her eyes, she saw trails of blue and yellow mist all around her. Then out of the blue and yellow mist there loomed an enormous dragon, the long coils of his body winding in and out among the tree tops while his savage head reared right up into the sky. But riding towards him across the sky, there came a knight in shining white armour on a winged white horse. The knight's golden sword flashed like a sunbeam and his cloak shimmered like moonlight as it streamed out behind him. There was a bright light on his forehead.

As he swung his sword, a strong wind began to blow, sweeping the leaves from the trees. The dragon cowered, drew back his head and sank among the blue and yellow mists.

When Sylvia went inside to have her lunch, she told her mother all about what Sister-in-the-Bushes had shown her, and then said:

"I would have felt really frightened of the dragon if Knight Michael hadn't been there."

Her mother answered:

"Yes, the dragon always tries to make us afraid, and Knight Michael's presence makes us brave. That was what Snowflake found when she saw the dragon."

Sylvia said:

"Oh, Mother, please tell me about Snowflake!"

And her mother promised:

"Tonight, then, in bed."

That night Sylvia chose Brian, her white toy pony, to take to bed with her because, even though he didn't have wings like the horse she had seen in the sky, she thought he was beautiful, swift and strong enough to be a brave knight's steed. When Sylvia and Brian were tucked up into bed, Sylvia's mother told them this story of Snowflake and the dragon:

The Story of Snowflake and the Dragon

One New Year's Eve, the Queen of the Moon was making snowflakes. Her three little daughters caught them as they fell from her fingers, and they laid them in a boat made of cloud. When the boat was filled, they breathed on it and set it drifting down to Earth. And as the first boat sailed away, another floated towards them to be filled.

As they came to lay the snowflakes in the second boat made of cloud, they all shouted out in surprise because at the bottom of the boat there slept a tiny child, made out of snow.

They all asked together:

"Mother, where is she going?"

The Queen of the Moon looked down at the Earth, and she told them:

"I can see a garden of lilies, and in the garden there is a palace of crystal roofed with silver. In the palace live a King and a

Queen who are waiting for a little daughter. This is their little daughter."

The first little princess said:

"We should give her a name before she goes."

The second little princess said:

"She is so white and small and lovely, she ought to be called Snowflake."

The third little princess said:

"Yes, let's call her Snowflake."

They gently covered her with snowflakes, and then they breathed on the boat made of cloud and sent it drifting down to Earth. They stood very still and quiet as they watched it float further and further away.

As soon as the boat reached the Earth, it scattered its snowflakes over the ground in a warm blanket, then went sailing on, taking the sleeping child of snow into a rocky cave.

Now in this cave lived nine good fairies and when they saw the gift which the boat made of cloud had brought them, they were very happy. They laid Snowflake gently in front of their fire, and warmed up some milk from their fairy cows ready for her when she would wake up.

When Snowflake awoke, she looked round her at the bright, warm fire and at the bright, kind faces of the nine good fairies, and she asked:

"Who are you? And please, can you tell me where am I?"

The nine good fairies answered:

"We are the nine fairy mothers and you have come from the Moon to stay with us in our cave for a little while."

So for nine months Snowflake lived in the cave with the nine fairy mothers and each fairy mother took a turn to look after her for a month while the others milked their fairy cows and made their fairy butter.

In the first month, which was January, the first fairy mother took care of Snowflake, and gave her snow with her fairy milk.

In the second month, which was February, the second fairy mother took care of Snowflake, and gave her dewdrops with her fairy milk.

In the third month, which was March, the third fairy mother took care of Snowflake, and gave her tree sap with her fairy milk.

In the fourth month, which was April, the fourth fairy mother took care of Snowflake, and gave her leaf buds with her fairy milk.

In the fifth month, which was May, the fifth fairy mother took care of Snowflake, and gave her fruit blossom with her fairy milk.

In the sixth month, which was June, the sixth fairy mother took care of Snowflake, and gave her pollen with her fairy milk.

In the seventh month, which was July, the seventh fairy mother took care of Snowflake, and gave her honey with her fairy milk.

In the eighth month, which was August, the eighth fairy mother took care of Snowflake, and gave her barley with her fairy milk.

In the ninth month, which was September, the ninth fairy mother took care of Snowflake, and gave her ripe red apples with her fairy milk.

As soon as Snowflake tasted the ripe red apples, she longed to leave the cave and see what the outside world was like. So one day, when the ninth fairy mother was away, fetching milk from the fairy cows, Snowflake began to creep along the narrow passage to where she could see daylight shining. When she reached the mouth of the cave, she saw that she was in a dazzling orchard. In the middle of the orchard there stood an apple tree, laden with ripe red apples. She ran to the apple tree, picked an apple, and began to eat it.

But when she began to look for a way out of the orchard, she couldn't find a way because a great dragon had coiled his long body all the way round the orchard. And all the time he was coming nearer and nearer.

The dragon said:

"I am going to eat you, Snowflake!"

Snowflake began to tremble. She ran back to the apple tree in the middle of the orchard and cried:

"Please save me from the dragon, apple tree!"

And the apple tree bent down its highest branches and lifted Snowflake right to the top of the tree.

But the dragon said:

"Do not think you can escape me that way, Snowflake! I can reach you even there!"

He was still coming closer and closer.

Snowflake looked to her right and to her left, in front of her and behind her, but she couldn't see any way to escape or anyone to save her.

Then the wind in the apple tree branches whispered:

"You have looked to your right and to your left and in front of you and behind you; but have you looked upwards, Snowflake?"

And when Snowflake looked upwards, she saw a noble knight in shining white armour riding swiftly across the sky above her head on a winged white horse. In his hand he held a glittering golden sword.

Snowflake called out loudly:

"White Knight, please save me from the dragon!"

The knight looked down and saw her in the apple tree, with the dragon coiling around its trunk as it reached up towards Snowflake, and he came riding swiftly down to Earth.

The dragon felt the wind as the knight swooped down, looked up and then quickly, very quickly, began to uncoil himself from the trunk of the apple tree. He cried out very humbly:

"Do not slay me, Knight Michael, and I will complete my task."

Knight Michael asked sternly:

"What is that task?"

The dragon answered, still very humbly:

"It is to bring Snowflake safely to the garden of lilies and to protect her while she lives upon the Earth."

Knight Michael looked up at Snowflake in the apple tree, and he said:

"Come down from the apple tree, Snowflake."

Snowflake came down from the apple tree but she was still very afraid.

Then Knight Michael put his golden sword into her hand and he said to her:

"If you thrust my sword into the dragon's side and slay him, he will not defend himself while I am near. But if instead you lay my sword upon his head, he will promise to serve you forever. It is your choice, Snowflake, what to do."

Then Snowflake looked at the dragon, at his fanged jaws and hideous body, and she shuddered and thought it would be better to slay him. Then she looked at his eyes, and they were so hopeless and unhappy that suddenly she felt sorry for him.

So she came towards him, slowly and still a little afraid of him. But the presence of Knight Michael gave her courage; and she stretched out her hand and laid the glittering golden sword on the dragon's head.

And at once a faint, dull light began to shine from the dragon, growing brighter and brighter until Snowflake saw that beneath his scales he had stars along his sides.

Now he looked so kind and friendly, and even beautiful with all his blazing stars, that Snowflake was no longer afraid of him, and sat upon his back without hesitation.

Knight Michael took back his golden sword and the dragon brought Snowflake safely to the garden of lilies. And in the middle of the garden was a palace of crystal roofed with silver. And the King and Queen came out of the palace. As soon as

Snowflake saw them she loved them both, and she ran to them and jumped into their arms.

So Snowflake became a princess and lived happily with the King and Queen in the palace of crystal roofed with silver within the garden of lilies.

And the dragon stayed with Snowflake to protect her all her life and they became the best of friends.

The Poem of Knight Michael

Before Sylvia and Brian went to sleep, Sylvia opened her Wonder Book, put it on the table, and softly chanted her poetry spell:

> "Rhyme-elves, rich in ringing words
> Won from winds and waves and birds,
> Lisping leaves and rustling rain,
> Sing – sing – for me again!"

When she woke next morning there was a new poem on a new page of the Wonder Book and beside it there was a picture of Knight Michael on his winged horse riding towards the dragon, his cloak streaming behind him and his sword lifted high. Sylvia bounced with excitement as she looked at it because in the picture Knight Michael's horse looked exactly like Brian, if only he had wings! She woke up Brian straight away to show him his portrait.

Then they took the Wonder Book into her mother's bed and this was the new poem her mother read to them:

Michael's sword
Is more burnished than a sunbeam;
Michael's mail
Is whiter than clear noon;
Michael's voice
Is majestic as the thunder;
Michael's cloak
Is brighter than the moon.
Michael's steed
Is swifter than a meteor;
Michael's brow
Is more radiant than the sky;
If my heart is more valiant
Than the dragon's might,
Michael's child
Am I.

Sylvia and the Old Woodsman

One afternoon a few days later, Sylvia heard the *clip – clop – clop* of Blackbird on the woodland path, bringing logs to her white cottage. She ran out and opened the gate so that the old woodsman could help Bluebird back in. Sylvia loved to help the old woodsman unload the logs. She climbed in and out of the cart picking up piles of logs of all different shapes and sizes to carry into the wood shed.

Sylvia thought how kind he was to bring the wood and carry it so carefully, in lovely neat piles, and she cried:

"Oh, Mr Woodsman, you are so kind to us! Why are you so kind to us?"

The old woodsman straightened his back, pushed back his old, old hat, and looked down at Sylvia standing looking up at him. Then he laughed his slow, cosy laugh, and said:

"Well now, one beast should help another, as the Lowly Ant said to the Lordly Cockerel!"

Then he went back to work, piling up the logs and Sylvie continued to help him as she puzzled over what to say next.

"One beast should help another, as the Lowly Ant said to the Lordly Cockerel!"

It was a strange but wonderful thing to say and she was quite, quite sure that it was the start of a good story.

So when they had finished stacking the logs, after they'd given Blackbird her sugar lump, and after they'd gone inside and washed their hands, the old woodsman sat down in front

43

of a fire made with the new logs while Sylvia's mother made tea. Sylvia came and stood between his knees, looked up into his kind, brown face, and asked:

"Mr Woodsman, please tell me why the Lowly Ant said that to the Lordly Cockerel? Is it a story?"

The old woodsman threw back his head and laughed his slow, cosy laugh, and picked Sylvia up and sat her down on his shiny brown corduroy knee. She leaned back against his homemade coat being tickled by its hairs and smelling its smell of trees and smoke and peat and woodland animals.

And the old woodsman said:

"Certainly it is a story! What a little greedy one you are for stories! All right – now just you listen, and I'll tell you!"

And in the slow, cosy voice that Sylvia loved, he told her the story of the Lordly Cockerel. And I wish you could have been sitting on the old woodsman's knee so you could have heard him telling it.

The Story of the Lordly Cockerel

There was once a Lordly Cockerel who was a proud and mighty hero. One sunny morning he was strutting about the farmyard in his fine feather trousers, pecking at seeds and insects, when he came upon a Lowly Ant struggling with a seed much bigger than herself.

The Lordly Cockerel exclaimed:

"Aha, Lowly Ant! I will eat your seed and you as well!"

Now although Lordly Cockerel was a very proud and mighty hero, Lowly Ant was not the least bit afraid of him and he answered calmly:

"*Do not* eat my seed, mighty hero, as the ant-hill babies need it. The ant-hill babies need me, too, so do not eat me either.

Instead, why don't you help me carry the seed to them because it's too big for me to manage all by myself."

This amused Lordly Cockerel, and he asked:

"Why should *I*, a mighty hero, carry the seed for *you*, a Lowly Ant?"

The Lowly Ant replied, as calmly as before:

"Because one beast should help another."

Hearing this, Lordly Cockerel laughed mightily, picked up the seed in his beak, and carried it to the ant-hill for Lowly Ant. When she thanked him, he gave her a proud and mighty bow, then went on strutting about the farmyard in his fine feather trousers.

Now just outside the farmyard gate, Wily Fox lay hidden in the long grass, watching Lordly Cockerel. As if out of nowhere Lordly Cockerel heard a voice murmuring:

"Won't you crow us the time of day, mighty hero? Perhaps you should stand on the farmyard gate, where everyone can see and admire you?"

When Lordly Cockerel heard such a flattering thing about himself he felt *very* proud and mighty so he flew up on to the farmyard gate, flapped his wings, and lifted up his voice in a proud and mighty:

"Cock-a-doodle-doo!"

Then the coaxing voice murmured again out of nowhere:

"Beau-ti-ful! But didn't you know, mighty hero, that the proudest and most mighty heroes crow with their eyes shut?"

So Lordly Cockerel flapped his wings and closed his eyes and lifted up his voice again in an even prouder and mightier:

"Cock-a-doodle-doo!"

And while his eyes were closed, Wily Fox pounced on him, tearing his fine feather trousers. With Lordly Cockerel held tightly between his teeth, he ran like the wind towards his distant den.

From her ant-hill Lowly Ant had seen Wily Fox steal away

Lordly Cockerel so she scurried as quickly as she could to see Lordly Cockerel's Favourite Hen, and told her:

"Favourite Hen, Wily Fox has caught our Lordly Cockerel, our proud and mighty hero, and torn his feather trousers, and carried him off to eat him!"

Then Favourite Hen called out to Duck:

"Duck, Lowly Ant says Wily Fox has caught our Lordly Cockerel, our proud and mighty hero, and torn his feather trousers, and carried him off to eat him!"

Then Duck called out to Goose:

"Goose, Favourite Hen says Lowly Ant says Wily Fox has caught our Lordly Cockerel, our proud and mighty hero, and torn his feather trousers, and carried him off to eat him!"

Then Goose called out to Dog:

"Dog, Duck says Favourite Hen says Lowly Ant says Wily Fox has caught our Lordly Cockerel, our proud and mighty hero, and torn his feather trousers, and carried him off to eat him!"

Then Dog called out to Sheep:

"Sheep, Goose says Duck says Favourite Hen says Lowly Ant says Wily Fox has caught our Lordly Cockerel, our proud and mighty hero, and torn his feather trousers, and carried him off to eat him!"

Then Sheep called out to Horse:

"Horse, Dog says Goose says Duck says Favourite Hen says Lowly Ant says Wily Fox has caught our Lordly Cockerel, our proud and mighty hero, and torn his feather trousers, and carried him off to eat him!"

Then Horse called out to Cow:

"Cow, Sheep says Dog says Goose says Duck says Favourite Hen says Lowly Ant says Wily Fox has caught our Lordly Cockerel, our proud and mighty hero, and torn his feather trousers, and carried him off to eat him!"

Then Cow called out to the milk maid:

"Milk maid, Horse says Sheep says Dog says Goose says Duck says Favourite Hen says Lowly Ant says Wily Fox has caught our Lordly Cockerel, our proud and mighty hero, and torn his feather trousers, and carried him off to eat him!"

Then the milk maid called out to the farmer:

"Farmer, Cow says Horse says Sheep says Dog says Goose says Duck says Favourite Hen says Lowly Ant says Wily Fox has caught our Lordly Cockerel, our proud and mighty hero, and torn his feather trousers, and carried him off to eat him!"

As soon as the farmer heard this, he opened the farmyard gate, and ran after Wily Fox; and the milk maid ran after the farmer; and Cow ran after the milk maid; and Horse ran after Cow; and Sheep ran after Horse; and Dog ran after Sheep; and Goose ran after Dog; and Duck ran after Goose; and Favourite Hen ran after Duck; and Lowly Ant came scurrying after them all.

The farmer shouted; and the milk maid screamed; and Cow mooed; and Horse neighed; and Sheep bleated; and Dog barked; and Goose cackled; and Duck quacked; and Favourite Hen clucked; and Lowly Ant couldn't make a sound because she was so out of breath after scurrying after them all.

Then Lordly Cockerel said to Wily Fox, as he hung between his jaws:

"You will never reach your den with me, Wily Fox! Can't you hear that the farmer and the milk maid and Cow and Horse and Sheep and Dog and Goose and Duck and Favourite Hen are close behind, while Lowly Ant is scurrying after them all?"

Wily Fox replied:

"Bah! I can *easily* outrun the farmer, the milk maid, Cow, Horse, Sheep, Dog, Goose, Duck, Favourite Hen, *and* Lowly Ant who is scurrying after them all!"

But while Wily Fox's mouth was open, saying this, Lordly Cockerel slipped from between his teeth, and flew into a tree.

When he reached the top he flapped his wings and lifted up his voice in the proudest, mightiest, most triumphant "Cock-a-doodle-doo!" you ever heard.

Then arrived the farmer and the milk maid and Cow and Horse and Sheep and Dog and Goose and Duck and Favourite Hen; and Lowly Ant came scurrying after them all. And Wily Fox slunk home to his den empty-handed.

Then Lordly Cockerel flew down from the tree and bowed his thanks to the farmer. And the farmer said:

"Don't thank *me*, Lordly Cockerel. Thank the milk maid. *She* told me."

Then Lordly Cockerel bowed his thanks to the milk maid. But the milk maid said:

"Don't thank *me*, Lordly Cockerel. Thank Cow. *She* told me."

Then Lordly Cockerel bowed his thanks to Cow. But Cow said:

"Don't thank *me*, Lordly Cockerel. Thank Horse. *He* told me."

Then Lordly Cockerel bowed his thanks to Horse. But Horse said:

"Don't thank *me*, Lordly Cockerel. Thank Sheep. *He* told me."

Then Lordly Cockerel bowed his thanks to Sheep. But Sheep said:

"Don't thank *me*, Lordly Cockerel. Thank Dog. *He* told me."

Then Lordly Cockerel bowed his thanks to Dog. But Dog said: 'Don't thank *me*, Lordly Cockerel. Thank Goose. *She* told me."

Then Lordly Cockerel bowed his thanks to Goose. But Goose said:

"Don't thank *me*, Lordly Cockerel. Thank Duck. *She* told me.

Then Lordly Cockerel bowed his thanks to Duck. But Duck said:

"Don't thank *me*, Lordly Cockerel. Thank Favourite Hen. *She* told me."

Then Lordly Cockerel bowed his thanks to Favourite Hen. But Favourite Hen said:

"Don't thank *me*, Lordly Cockerel. Thank Lowly Ant. *She* told me."

Then Lordly Cockerel bowed his thanks to Lowly Ant. And Lowly Ant waved her front legs politely, and said:

"Don't mention it, Lordly Cockerel. One beast should help another."

Then Favourite Hen said to Lordly Cockerel:

"And now my mighty hero, come home because those trousers need mending!"

The Poem of Wily, Lordly and Lowly

That night Sylvia took all her farmyard animals – her cow and Brian and her sheep and Pip and her goose and her duck and her cockerel and her hen – to bed with her. She put her Wonder Book on her bedside table, and she softly chanted her poetry spell:

> "Rhyme-elves, rich in ringing words
> Won from winds and waves and birds,
> Lisping leaves and rustling rain,
> Sing – sing – for me again!"

And next morning, when she woke up, she saw a new poem and a new picture on a new page. First she looked at the new picture, and chuckled over the portrait of Lordly Cockerel in his fine feather trousers. Then she took her Wonder Book, and all her farmyard animals too, into her mother's bed. And this was the new poem her mother read to them all:

Wily has a heart of stone.
He walks his woodland ways alone.
Alone he fares, alone he feasts:
He knows no brotherhood of beasts.
O Wily Fox!
If your cold heart should yearn to find
Kind fellowship, *you* must be kind,
Poor Wily!

Lordly is a sultan proud.
His comb glares red, and his voice crows
    loud.
He struts with pomp and glances grim.
His feather trousers flaunt on him.
O Lordly Cockerel!
Your bluff heart yet can learn that kings
Are kith and kin with creeping things,
Vain Lordly!

Lowly is small and black as soot,
And big beasts tread her underfoot;
Yet ever brave and brisk is she
To aid them in adversity.
O Lowly Ant!
As wakefully your ways you wend,
You are the whole world's tiny friend,
Dear Lowly!

Sylvia's Turnip Lantern

On the last night of October there was going to be a Hallowe'en Party in the village, and after dark all the children were to parade with their lighted Hallowe'en lanterns made out of hollowed-out turnips. So that morning, after Sylvia had helped her mother to sweep and dust, she asked:

"Shall I run into the garden now, Mother, and get a turnip for my lantern?"

And her mother said:

"Do you think you can pull it up all by yourself?"

And Sylvia answered:

"I'm sure I can!"

So Sylvia ran into the garden, and looked at all the turnips, and chose the one with the biggest leaves, and began to pull and pull. But the turnip tucked its head into the earth and did not move. So Sylvia took a deep breath and pulled again. But the turnip still didn't move. Then she took a deeper breath, and pulled and pulled again. And suddenly she sat down backwards with a bump, with a big, white, chubby turnip in her hands.

She took it inside and carefully washed it and dried it. Then her mother helped her to scrape out the insides and carve a face with a long, curved, smiling mouth on the outside. Sylvia put a candle inside, and lit it, and stood it in a dark cupboard, to see what it would look like at the party.

The candlelight shone soft and rosy inside the turnip head, turning it into a beautiful lantern. And inside her own head

51

Sylvia imagined all those rosy lanterns – hers and Joan's and Terry's and Rosaleen's and Margaret's and Luke's and Stephen's – bobbing through the darkness along the village street.

Sylvia said to her mother:

"The turnip looks so lovely now that it must be glad it let me pull it up. At first it didn't want to come at all."

Her mother smiled and said:

"Perhaps you didn't pull it up in the right way."

Sylvia's eyes opened wide in surprise, and she asked:

"What do you mean Mother? Is there a right way and a wrong way to pull up a turnip?"

Her mother answered:

"Hugin found there was when he tried to pull up his turnip."

Sylvia exclaimed:

"Oh, Mother, is it a story? Please tell me!"

So while her mother scraped and carved a little more here and there inside the turnip to make the lantern even lighter, and made the smiling face outside the turnip even more smiling, she told Sylvia the story of Hugin and the turnip.

And this is it:

The Story of Hugin and the Turnip

Once upon a time there was a little boy named Hugin, and he wanted a turnip to make a Hallowe'en lantern, so he went out into the garden and planted a turnip seed; and he said:

> "Turnip, Turnip, grow for me;
> Grow as big as big can be,
> That I may make for Hallowe'en
> The finest lantern ever seen.
> I-want-to-put-a-candle-in-you, Turnip."

So the turnip grew as big as big could be, till it was so big that it nearly filled the garden.

Then Hugin went out to pull the turnip up. And he pulled and he pulled; but the turnip wouldn't budge an inch.

Just then a lion came by, and asked:

"What are you doing, Hugin?"

And Hugin replied:

"I'm pulling up a turnip.

> Lion, Lion, pull with me;
> Pull as hard as hard can be,
> That I may make for Hallowe'en
> The finest lantern ever seen.
> I-want-to-put-a-candle-in-my-turnip."

So Lion pulled Hugin, and Hugin pulled the turnip. They pulled and they pulled, but the turnip wouldn't budge an inch.

Just then a bear came along, and asked:

"What are you doing, Lion?"

And the lion replied:

"I'm helping Hugin to pull up a turnip."

And Hugin said:

> "Bear, Bear, pull with me;
> Pull as hard as hard can be,
> That I may make for Hallowe'en
> The finest lantern ever seen.
> I-want-to-put-a-candle-in-my-turnip."

So Bear pulled Lion, and Lion pulled Hugin, and Hugin pulled the turnip. They pulled and they pulled, but the turnip wouldn't budge an inch.

Just then a fox came by, and asked:

"What are you doing, Bear?"

And the bear replied:

"I'm helping Lion to help Hugin to pull up a turnip."

And Hugin said:

> "Fox, Fox, pull with me;
> Pull as hard as hard can be,
> That I may make for Hallowe'en
> The finest lantern ever seen.
> I-want-to-put-a-candle-in-my-turnip."

So Fox pulled Bear, and Bear pulled Lion, and Lion pulled Hugin, and Hugin pulled the turnip. They pulled and they pulled, but the turnip wouldn't budge an inch.

Just then a hare came by, and asked:

"What are you doing, Fox?"

And the fox replied:

"I'm helping Bear to help Lion to help Hugin to pull up a turnip."

And Hugin said:

> "Hare, Hare, pull with me;
> Pull as hard as hard can be,
> That I may make for Hallowe'en
> The finest lantern ever seen.
> I-want-to-put-a-candle-in-my-turnip."

So Hare pulled Fox, and Fox pulled Bear, and Bear pulled Lion, and Lion pulled Hugin, and Hugin pulled the turnip. They pulled and they pulled, but the turnip wouldn't budge an inch.

Just then a mouse came by, and asked:

"What are you doing, Hare?"

And the hare replied:

"I'm helping Fox to help Bear to help Lion to help Hugin to pull up a turnip."

And Hugin said:

> "Mouse, Mouse, pull with me;
> Pull as hard as hard can be,
> That I may make for Hallowe'en
> The finest lantern ever seen.
> I-want-to-put-a-candle-in-my-turnip."

So Mouse pulled Hare, and Hare pulled Fox, and Fox pulled Bear, and Bear pulled Lion, and Lion pulled Hugin, and Hugin pulled the turnip. They pulled and they pulled, but the turnip wouldn't budge an inch.

Just then a caterpillar came by, and asked:

"What are you doing, Mouse?"

And the mouse replied:

"I'm helping Hare to help Fox to help Bear to help Lion to help Hugin to pull up a turnip."

And Caterpillar said:

"But does Hugin know the right way to pull up a turnip? Did he remember to ask its root gnome if he could first?"

Surprised, Hugin bent down and put his mouth close to the ground, and called:

> "Gnome, gnome, good root gnome,
> May I take your turnip home,
> That I may make for Hallowe'en
> The finest lantern ever seen?
> I-want-to-put-a-candle-in-your-turnip."

Suddenly a little root gnome popped his brown head up out of the ground, and said:

"Good gracious me, Hugin, why didn't you *ask* me? All this

time I've been pulling the other way, when there's nothing a root gnome likes better than a candle put in his turnip! Now pull again!"

And he popped his brown head back into the ground.

So Caterpillar pulled Mouse, and Mouse pulled Hare, and Hare pulled Fox, and Fox pulled Bear, and Bear pulled Lion, and Lion pulled Hugin, and Hugin pulled the turnip. And suddenly Mouse sat down backwards with a bump on Caterpillar, and Hare sat down backwards with a bump on Mouse, and Fox sat down backwards with a bump on Hare, and Bear sat down backwards with a bump on Fox, and Lion sat down backwards with a bump on Bear, and Hugin sat down backwards with a bump on Lion, with the biggest, whitest, chubbiest turnip in his hand that anyone had ever seen!

Then Hugin got up and said "sorry" to Lion; and Lion got up and said "sorry" to Bear; and Bear got up and said "sorry" to Fox; and Fox got up and said "sorry" to Hare; and Hare got up and said "sorry" to Mouse; and Mouse got up and said "sorry" to Caterpillar. And nobody was hurt, and everybody laughed, and Hugin put-a-candle-in-his-turnip.

The Poem of Hallowe'en Lanterns

The Hallowe'en party was just as exciting as Sylvia had hoped, and the parade of rosy lanterns along the dark village street was even more beautiful than Sylvia imagined it would be.

When the party was over, the old woodsman came with Blackbird to take Sylvia home; and she was so happily tired that she fell asleep on the way with her face buried in the tickling hairs of his old coat. She woke up just enough to get undressed; and when her mother had tucked her up in bed, she was only just awake enough to remember to put her Wonder Book beside her turnip-lantern on the bedside table, and to chant her poetry spell very sleepily –

> "Rhyme-elves rich in ringing words
> Won from winds and waves and birds,
> Lisping leaves and rustling rain,
> Sing – sing – for me again!" –

before she fell sound asleep again.

The next morning, when she woke up, refreshed after a good night's sleep, her Wonder Book was open at a new page, and there was a new picture of Hugin and Lion and Bear and Fox and Hare and Mouse and Caterpillar all pulling up the big turnip. She sat up in bed and laughed out loud. And when she took the Wonder Book into her mother's bed, this was the new poem her mother read to her:

> Beautiful are forests when the leaves are green;
> Beautiful are rainbows where a storm has
>   been;
> Beautiful are lanterns in the night at
>   Hallowe'en.
>
> Beautiful are lanterns gilding spring's bright
>   shoots;
> Beautiful are lanterns firing autumn's fruits;
> Beautiful are lanterns carved from winter's
>   earthy roots.
>
> Hallowe'en lanterns swinging soft and slow;
> Hallowe'en lanterns filled with candle-glow –
> Gently shining candles, cupped in caves of
>   rosy snow.

Vegetable faces in a flickering file
Shimmer in the darkness, sway and pause
    awhile,
On each brow a brightness, and a star behind
    each smile.

Sylvia and the Wicked Little Imp

One grey November afternoon, Sylvia was swinging on the garden gate while she waited for her mother to come back from the village, when suddenly a bouncing little voice called out:

"Hello, Sylvia!"

And there, peeping from behind a tree trunk in the dark wood, she saw a little imp.

Sylvia said in surprise:

"Can you really see me? The earth knights said they can't see me until I'm seven."

The little imp jumped up, snapped his little fingers, and said disdainfully:

"They're only *ordinary* fairies. I can do *lots* of things they can't."

Sylvia was very impressed by this, and said respectfully:

"Can you really? Please come into the garden and show me what you can do."

But the little imp shuddered, and said:

"Not I. I just can't stand being inside a nut hedge."

Now that should have warned Sylvia that the little imp was not the sort of fairy she should be talking to because the old woodsman had told her that the reason wise people planted nut hedges round their gardens was to keep bad goblins out. She also should have been warned by what the little imp said next. He said:

"Why don't you come into the dark wood instead?"

Sylvia told him:

"I'm not allowed to go there alone."

The little imp tried to persuade her:

"But you wouldn't be alone. You'd be with me."

Sylvia hadn't wanted to go into the dark wood without her mother before the little imp suggested it but now she really wanted to go, so she said hopefully:

"Perhaps Mother wouldn't mind me going without her if Sister-in-the-Bushes came instead."

But the little imp made an ugly face, and said meanly:

"Oh no – don't ask *her*. It would be much more fun if it was just the two of us. I know a secret place where you can find the most gorgeous spotted toadstools."

Sylvia asked:

"Could I bring some home for my mother?"

And the little imp answered:

"Of course you could – as many as you like."

For some reason Sylvia thought that made the idea seem not quite so naughty so she opened the gate, and went out into the dark wood with the little imp skipping in front.

At first he made it seem like a great adventure. He took Sylvia to a part of the dark wood she had never seen before, where yellow and scarlet and purple-spotted toadstools grew at the foot of the pines; and he showed her how to plant them in damp moss to make a little garden. And Sylvia picked them till both her pockets were almost full.

Then she realised that it was almost teatime so she said politely:

"Thank you *very* much, but it's time I went home now."

But the little imp said:

"Oh, don't go yet, Sylvia. There's lots more to do and see. Let's go along *this* path."

And Sylvia was just about to follow him when a soft voice whispered in her ear:

"Don't go, Sylvia. That's the path to the bog."

Sylvia couldn't see anybody, but she knew the voice belonged to Sister-in-the Bushes. So she called:

"Oh no, little imp. I'm too tired."

So the little imp turned back, and suggested:

"Then let's sit down a bit on this soft moss."

Sylvia was very glad to sit down because suddenly she was feeling very weak and tired and she was also pretty sure that it was teatime so she exclaimed:

"Oh dear, I'm *so* hungry!"

And the little imp said:

"Then why not eat a nice toadstool? They're really very tasty. Look – have this one!"

And he picked a brilliant scarlet one growing close beside him.

Sylvia was so hungry that she took it and was just going to bite into it when Sister-in-the-Bushes' soft voice whispered again in her ear:

"Don't eat it, Sylvia. It's poisonous."

So Sylvia said:

"No, thank you, little imp. I'd like to go home now, please."

Then the little imp looked at her, and grinned wickedly, and said:

"But do you know your way? I don't. Look at all these paths – don't they all look the same?"

It was true. All the paths did look the same. Sylvia had a feeling that the wicked little imp was making fun of her and she began to cry. By now dusk was creeping through the dark wood, and she was frightened that she'd still be lost in the woods when it got cold and dark.

Then the little imp suggested:

"Why not come home with *me*?"

Sylvia was so worried about being alone in the dark wood all night that she was just about to get up and follow him when the soft voice whispered again:

"Don't go home with the wicked little imp, Sylvia. He lives in a deep, dark pool. But be brave. Your mother will soon be here."

Sylvia looked round again and this time she was sure she saw the faint white figure of Sister-in-the-Bushes moving between the tree trunks. So she dried her eyes; and no matter what pleasant thing the little imp suggested, she refused to move, even though the evening shadows grew thicker all the time.

Then, from far away, she heard her mother's voice calling faintly:

"Sylvia! Sylvia!"

And Sylvia jumped up and called back:

"I'm here, Mother! Oh, Mother, Mother!"

And then again she saw the faint white figure of Sister-in-the-Bushes, but this time moving towards her. Following Sister-in-the-Bushes Sylvia saw a lantern flickering in and out among the trees and she ran as fast as she could towards it, and threw herself, sobbing, sobbing, into her mother's arms.

Her mother kissed her and comforted her, and didn't tell her off all the way home.

When they reached their white cottage, Sylvia was so tired that her mother said she could have tea in bed as a special treat. Sylvia got undressed and sat up in bed, with Kate, the old baby doll, snuggling into one side of her, and Titania, the fairy doll, snuggling into the other, and a hot-water bottle warming her cold toes. Then her mother came in with warm milk and hot buttered toast and Sylvia threw her arms round her and cried:

"Oh, Mother, I love you so much!"

Sylvia's mother stroked her tangled curls away from her forehead, and said: "You should never do what a wicked little imp wants you to do again, Sylvia, especially if he doesn't want Sister-in-the-Bushes to do it, too."

Sylvia opened her eyes wide in surprise, and asked:

"*How* did you know about the little imp, Mother?"

And her mother answered:

62

"Whenever anyone doesn't do what they are told it is always because they have let a wicked little imp persuade them. That was how the youngest prince came to grow that ugly long nose."

Feeling much, much better at the idea of another story, Sylvia begged:

"Oh, Mother, please tell me about him!"

So when Sylvia had finished her warm milk and her hot buttered toast, and had snuggled down into bed between Kate and Titania and the hot-water bottle, her mother sat on the edge of the bed and told them the story of the Country at the Bottom of the Well.

And here it is:

The Story of the Country at the Bottom of the Well

The King of the shining Land of the Sun had three sons. Two of them worked hard, learning how to become kings themselves. But the youngest prince said to his father:

"Father, I do not want to learn how to become a king. I only want to wander about the kingdom, seeing new sights and people."

And the King replied:

"My son, you shall be free to wander for a year and a day. At the end of that time, return to the palace, and we will speak further on these matters."

And he gave the youngest prince five animals to be his friends and companions on his journey – an elephant, a giraffe, a stork, a monkey and a stoat. And the King said to the five animals:

"Whatever the youngest prince does, you must do. And wherever the youngest prince goes, you must go."

And to the youngest prince he gave this warning:

"Everything in the shining Land of the Sun is beautiful, and everything there except one thing is good. That is the silver cherry tree. If you find it, beware that you do not pick and eat any of its cherries, or they will lead you to disaster."

Then the youngest prince set out with his friends, the five animals. And each new thing he saw in the shining Land of the Sun was more beautiful than the last, until, in a hidden valley far away from anywhere, he came upon the silver cherry tree, its branches heavy with glittering silver cherries. And he thought that this was the most beautiful thing of all.

When the youngest prince and the five animals came close to the silver cherry tree, to admire it, they found that there was a well at its roots. And as they leaned over it and gazed down into its dark depths, the youngest prince remarked:

"I can see no water. I wonder what is at the bottom?"

And at once a hollow voice from a long, long distance down replied:

"My kingdom lies at the bottom of the well."

And the youngest prince exclaimed in surprise:

"I'd love to see a country at the bottom of a well!"

And the hollow voice replied:

"That is quite easy. All you have to do is to eat a silver cherry."

Then the youngest prince sighed and said:

"But the King my father has forbidden me to do that."

And the hollow voice replied:

"There is no other way."

Now the youngest prince longed to see the Country at the Bottom of the Well, because he loved seeing new things. So he ignored his father's warning, and he said to the five animals:

"I am going to eat a silver cherry. Will you eat one with me?"

And the elephant and the giraffe and the stork and the monkey and the stoat answered together:

"Whatever the youngest prince does, we will do.
Wherever the youngest prince goes, we will go."

So the youngest prince reached up to the silver cherry tree, and he picked a bunch of six silver cherries, and he gave one to each of the animals, and kept one for himself. Each of them ate their silver cherry, and they placed the six cherry stones in a ring at the foot of the tree.

Suddenly the wind started to blow, caught them up, and whirled them – prince, elephant, giraffe, stork, monkey, stoat – down, down, down into the darkness, and set them on their feet in the Country at the Bottom of the Well.

After the brightness and the beauty of the shining Land of the Sun, the Country at the Bottom of the Well seemed to them to be very dark and wild and ugly. The light was grey because no sun was shinning and there were no flowers, but everywhere there were marshes and old mine shafts and steep cliffs and ravines.

As the youngest prince and the five animals looked around them in horror, they heard mocking laughter behind them and turned around to see the King of that country coming towards them wearing a crown of lead with his courtiers close behind him. And the King was a wicked imp. And all his courtiers were wicked imps, too.

And the King of the Wicked Imps shouted:

"Welcome, Prince Long-Nose!"

And all the wicked imps laughed mockingly.

Then the King of the Wicked Imps shouted again:

"Welcome, Elephant Finger-Face, Giraffe Head-in-Air, Stork Spindle-Shanks, Monkey Flapping-Sleeves, Stoat Snake-Body!"

And all the wicked imps laughed mockingly again.

Now every person and every animal in the shining Land of the Sun was beautiful so the youngest prince and the five animals looked at one another in surprise, wondering what the King of the Wicked Imps could mean.

But they found that what the King said was true. The beautiful young prince had grown a long, long nose; the elephant had

grown a long finger on his face; the giraffe's neck had shot up until his head was lifted far away; the stork's legs had lengthened into two tall, bony stilts; the monkey's arms hung to the ground like sleeves that needed shortening; and the stoat's body had stretched lengthways till he did look rather like a snake on legs.

And the youngest prince and the five animals all began to ache all over with their new ugliness.

Then the youngest prince cried in dismay:

"What can have made us all so ugly – so ugly that we ache all over with it?"

And the King of the Wicked Imps answered gloatingly:

"Eating the silver cherries has done that."

Then the youngest prince said arrogantly:

"I have seen enough of this Country at the Bottom of the Well. I wish to return to the shining Land of the Sun now."

But the King of the Wicked Imps laughed mockingly again, and told him:

"You will never see the sun again, Prince Long-Nose. For the only way to climb to the top of the well is by a secret stair; and nothing except the golden pear can lead you to the secret stair. But the golden pear is so cunningly hidden that you'll never find it and even if you did, my wicked imps would steal it from you."

Now all Prince Long-Nose wanted was to find the golden pear so he and the five animals began to wander all over the Country at the Bottom of the Well, searching for it. They wandered through marshy regions, and they wandered through regions of old mine shafts, and they wandered through regions of cliffs and ravines but they couldn't find the golden pear anywhere.

Since the prince had grown his ugly long nose he could smell things that his beautiful short nose would never have noticed. One day, as he and the five animals were passing the mouth of a small cave, his long nose twitched. He paused and twitched it again, then cried in excitement:

"I can smell pears!"

So, following the pear scent, he led the five animals into the cave and further and further in along a narrow rocky passage. After a while they saw a light ahead of them brighter than any light they had yet seen in this dark country. When they reached the end of the passage, they stepped out into a desolate plain, on which nothing grew except one solitary tree in the middle. The gleaming, shinning tree lit up the whole desolate plain.

Prince Long-Nose and the five animals rushed across the empty plain to the gleaming tree and they found it was the golden pear tree they had been searching for, and on it there hung one solitary gleaming, golden pear.

Filled with thankfulness and joy, Prince Long-Nose picked the golden pear. It slipped through his fingers to the ground, and began to move as if attached to an invisible thread, leading them back to the bottom of the well.

They followed it over rough hills, till they came into a region of old mineshafts when suddenly, out of nowhere, a wicked imp pounced upon the golden pear, ran with it to the nearest mineshaft, and flung it in as hard as he could. Prince Long-Nose watched in dismay and so did Elephant Finger-Face, Giraffe Head-in-Air, Stork Spindle-Shanks, and Monkey Flapping-Sleeves.

But Stoat Snake-Body bowed and said:

"Let me get it, youngest prince!"

And into the mineshaft he went, his long body burrowing while the others held their breath as they waited. A moment later he came back, and in his mouth was the golden pear.

Then again the golden pear slipped to the ground and began to move as if attached to an invisible thread, leading them back to the bottom of the well.

They followed it through thorny thickets, till they came into a region of narrow passes winding between steep ravines. And suddenly, out of nowhere, a second wicked imp pounced upon the golden pear, ran with it to the nearest ravine, and threw it over as hard as he could. When the prince and the animals looked over the edge, they could see the golden pear gleaming far, far below like a fallen star. Prince Long-Nose stared down at it in dismay; and so did Elephant Finger-Face, Giraffe Head-in-Air, Stork Spindle-Shanks and Stoat Snake-Body.

But Monkey Flapping-Sleeves bowed and said:

"Let me get it, youngest prince!"

And over the edge he went, down the steep walls of the ravine, clinging on with his long arms to every piece of jutting rock and every trailing vine. The others held their breath as they waited. After a moment he came up and over the edge and in his mouth was the golden pear.

Then again the golden pear slipped to the ground, and began to move as if attached to an invisible thread, leading them back to the bottom of the well.

They followed it across bleak moors, till they came into a region of dangerous marshes. And suddenly, out of nowhere, a third wicked imp pounced upon the golden pear, ran with it to the edge of the nearest marsh, and threw it into it as hard as he could. The deep mud swallowed the golden pear, leaving nothing to mark the spot where it had disappeared.

Prince Long-Nose stared at the marsh in dismay; and so did Elephant Finger-Face, Giraffe Head-in-Air, Monkey Flapping-Sleeves and Stoat Snake-Body.

But Stork Spindle-Shanks bowed and said:

"Let me get it, youngest prince!"

And into the marsh he waded, his long, bony stilts of legs carrying him safely through the deep mud, which his long beak stabbed here, there, and everywhere. The others held their breath as they waited. After a moment he came back, and in his beak was the golden pear.

Then again the golden pear slipped to the ground, and began to move as if attached to an invisible thread, leading them back to the bottom of the well.

They followed it between barren mountains, till they came to a region of tall cliffs and deep gorges. And suddenly, out of nowhere, a fourth wicked imp pounced upon the golden pear and ran with it up the side of the nearest tall cliff, and tossed it into the nest of a bird of prey on one of the cliff's high ledges. The fledglings in the nest began to scream, and the angry parent birds circled threateningly round the prince and his animals below, ready to attack if they tried to climb the cliff. Prince Long-Nose stared at them in dismay; and so did Elephant Finger-Face, Stork Spindle-Shanks, Monkey Flapping-Sleeves and Stoat Snake-Body.

But Giraffe Head-in-Air bowed and said:

"Let me get it, youngest prince!"

And high above the circling birds of prey he lifted his long neck, and darted his head into the nest as the fledglings screamed. The others held their breath as they waited. After a moment he bent his long neck again, and between his lips was the golden pear.

Then again the golden pear slipped to the ground, and began to move as if attached to an invisible thread, leading them back to the bottom of the well.

They followed it across a dreary desert until they could just see the bottom of the well in the distance when suddenly, out of nowhere, a fifth wicked imp pounced upon the golden pear, and ran with it into a crack between rocks which was far to small for anyone but a wicked imp to enter.

Prince Long-Nose stared at the crevice in dismay; and so did Giraffe Head-in-Air, Stork Spindle-Shanks, Monkey Flapping-Sleeves and Stoat Snake-Body.

But Elephant Finger-Face bowed and said:

"Let me get it, youngest prince!"

And he marched forward, trumpeting loudly, swinging his long trunk; and with it he pulled the rocks apart and searched for the pear. The others held their breath as they waited. After a moment he came back, and tucked safely into the end of his trunk was the golden pear.

Then again the golden pear slipped to the ground, and began to move as if attached to an invisible thread. It moved to the bottom of the well where the rock opened revealing a secret stair inside the wall of the well. The golden pear began to move up the secret stair; and Prince Long-Nose and Elephant Finger-Face and Giraffe Head-in-Air and Stork Spindle-Shanks and Monkey Flapping-Sleeves and Stoat Snake-Body followed it. And the rock closed again behind them, shutting the wicked imps out.

At the top of the well they came out into the warmth and the golden light and the green grass and the beauty of the shining Land of the Sun. And there, under the silver cherry tree, stood the prince's father in his golden crown and his royal robes, gazing sadly at the ring of six cherry stones. The year and a day he had given the prince for his wandering had passed long ago and the King had been searching throughout his kingdom for him. When he found the six cherry stones under the silver cherry tree, he had feared that his youngest son was lost to him forever.

Overjoyed at seeing his son safe, the King wrapped Prince Long-Nose in his arms. Then he noticed the prince's long nose, and the elephant's long trunk, and the giraffe's long neck, and the stork's long legs, and the monkey's long arms, and the stoat's long body, so he set the golden pear upright in the middle of the ring of cherry stones. The golden pear fell into six pieces as cleanly as if you had cut it with a knife and each piece covered a cherry stone.

To Prince Long-Nose and each of the five animals, the King gave a piece of the golden pear to eat. And after they had eaten it they were no longer Prince Long-Nose and Elephant Finger-Face and Giraffe Head-in-Air and Stork Spindle-Shanks and Monkey Flapping-Sleeves and Stoat Snake-Body. They became as beautiful as they had been before they ate the silver cherries. And in the same moment they all stopped aching all over.

And the youngest prince exclaimed:

"Father, I am tired of wandering. I want to learn how to be a king!"

Then they all went back to the palace, where a rich banquet was prepared for them. And the King and the three young princes and the five beautiful animals all sat down to the banquet, and enjoyed the feast together.

The Poem of the Silver Cherry and the Golden Pear

When Sylvia's mother had finished the story, Sylvia felt so sleepy that, even though it was only just after teatime, she put out her Wonder Book right away and softly chanted her poetry spell:

> "Rhyme-elves, rich in ringing words
> Won from winds and waves and birds,
> Lisping leaves and rustling rain,
> Sing – sing – for me again!"

No sooner had her mother tucked Sylvia and Kate and Titania and the hot-water bottle into bed, and taken the tea tray, and turned out the light, than Sylvia went as fast asleep as if it were really bedtime.

She slept so well, even after her rather scary adventure with the wicked imp, that when she woke up it was morning, and she felt happy and rested. And there, on a new page of the Wonder Book, was a happy picture of the youngest prince and the five animals, finding the golden pear tree. When Sylvia and Kate and Titania took the Wonder Book into Sylvia's mother's bed, this was the new poem she read out to them:

> O youngest prince!
> This silver cherry in your hand
> Will lay on you a hideous spell,
> And drive you from the sun, to dwell
> In the wild, ugly, sunless land
> At the black bottom of the well.
>
> O youngest prince!
> Follow the gracious golden pear
> That lights up all this desolate plain;
> And it shall heal you of your pain,
> And lead you up the secret stair
> Back to your shining home again.

Sylvia's Advent Wreath

One frosty morning right at the end of November, Sylvia's mother said:

"Only a month now till Christmas, Sylvia! Shall we go into the wood today, and get the pine branches for our Advent wreath?"

So out they went along the woodland path. After her adventure with the wicked imp, Sylvia had been worried that she wouldn't be able to love the dark wood again. But she found out she loved it just as much as ever and today she did not even think of the wicked imp once.

Sylvia and her mother came home carrying lots of pine branches, which they twisted round a hoop of wire to make a thick green wreath. Then they added four tall white candles to the wreath, and hung it from the ceiling of the cottage living room with a long loop of broad red ribbon.

When it was dark and the curtains were drawn, Sylvia's mother lifted Sylvia up to the green wreath with a lighted taper, so that she could light the first candle. Next week there would be two candles lit every evening, and the next week three, till every evening of the last week before Christmas all four would be softly shining.

Sylvia sat on the hearth in front of the blazing log fire, and leaned back happily against her mother's knee, and looked up at the gentle candle glow falling on the red ribbon and the dark green wreath. She said:

"It's like an evergreen crown, isn't it, Mother, with a jewel in the candle flame?"

And her mother replied:

"That's why Rufusi Ryneker wanted to wear it so much."

And Sylvia exclaimed:

"Rufusi Ryneker? What a wonderful name! Who was he, Mother?"

So, sitting quietly in the firelight and the candle light, Sylvia's mother told her the story of Rufusi Ryneker.

And this is the story:

The Story of Rufusi Ryneker

There was once a fox with a fine red coat. His name was Rufusi Ryneker, which is a fine name for a fox. But the finest thing about him was his fine red brush; his wonderful tail.

Rufusi Ryneker's fine red brush was very clever. When Rufusi Ryneker was being hunted, his fine red brush helped him to escape, for it stretched out behind him and balanced his long body, so that he could swiftly swerve and change his direction, leaving the hounds and the huntsmen far behind.

And when it was Rufusi Ryneker himself who was hunting, his fine red brush helped him too. Rufusi Ryneker would lie hidden in the long grasses with his fine red brush waving about with the tip just showing and all the little curious birds, and especially the larks, would come flying close to discover what this waving red plume was; and in this way the fine red brush brought Rufusi Ryneker many delicious dinners.

One day when Rufusi Ryneker was lying hidden in the grass and his fine red brush was catching larks for his dinner, Rufusi Ryneker heard the blowing of the hunting horns and the shouts of the huntsmen and the baying of the hounds.

So up and away he went like a streak of glossy red lightning.

He twisted and turned across the countryside, his fine red brush helping him, till he came to a river, and swam across to the other side. It was a very muddy river, and he came ashore in a very muddy place.

Just then the blowing of the horns and the shouts of the huntsmen and the baying of the hounds told him that they had crossed the river too. So Rufusi Ryneker began to run again. But now he found that his fine red brush was heavy with water and mud, so that instead of stretching out behind and helping him, it kept dragging on the ground.

Rufusi Ryneker came to a forest, and entered it, hoping he might escape by twisting and turning among the trees; but the shouting huntsmen and the baying hounds were now so near that he knew they'd overtake him soon. And then, just as he lost heart, suddenly a little house with a green door appeared in the forest path in front of him. A little man stood holding the green door open. The little man waved at him, and called:

"Rufusi Ryneker! Come in quickly!"

Rufusi Ryneker ran through the open green door, and the little man snapped it shut, and stamped three times, and chanted:

> "Down, little house,
> Below the ground!
> Down, little house;
> Be no more found!"

And immediately the little house sank down right into the earth, and the forest path closed over its roof as if it were not there.

When Rufusi Ryneker had got his breath back, he began to look round the little house, and he saw that hanging by red ribbons from the painted ceiling was a crown of pine branches, and on the crown of pine branches were four lighted white candles with pure golden flames, and at the heart of each golden flame there shone a jewel.

Rufusi Ryneker looked at the crown of pine branches with joy, and with joy, and with great joy.

And he asked:

"Whose is this crown of candles, and why does it hang here?"

And the little man replied:

"It comes down from the skies, and it hangs here because this is the House of Crowning. I am All-Wise the Dwarf, and every winter I search among all the creatures in the forest, and when I have found the wisest, I crown him with this crown; and if he really is the wisest, then the gems in the flames of the candles will light up his head."

Then Rufusi Ryneker looked again at the crown with joy, and with joy, and with great joy; and he wanted nothing more than to be crowned with it.

And he said:

"Oh, All-Wise, I am wise. I am sure I must be the wisest of all the creatures in the forest!"

Then All-Wise the Dwarf looked at Rufusi Ryneker; and he answered:

"You are very, very clever, Rufusi Ryneker. But are you really wise? For instance, do you know whose fault it was that the hounds almost caught you today?"

Then Rufusi Ryneker asked his four feet:

"Four feet, my servants, was it your fault that the hounds almost caught me today?"

And Rufusi Ryneker's four feet answered:

"No, Rufusi Ryneker. We carried you swiftly and surely, as we always do."

Then Rufusi Ryneker asked his two eyes:

"Two eyes, my servants, was it your fault that the hounds almost caught me today?"

And Rufusi Ryneker's two eyes answered:

"No, Rufusi Ryneker. We were very watchful, as we always are."

Then Rufusi Ryneker asked his two ears:

"Two ears, my servants, was it your fault that the hounds almost caught me today?"

And Rufusi Ryneker's two ears answered:

"No, Rufusi Ryneker. As always, we were wide open and listening hard."

Then Rufusi Ryneker asked his fine red brush:

"Red brush, my servant, was it your fault that the hounds almost caught me today?"

And Rufusi Ryneker's fine red brush answered:

"Yes, Rufusi Ryneker. I dragged on the ground."

Then Rufusi Ryneker was furious with his fine red brush, and he cried to All-Wise the Dwarf:

"Give me your knife, All-Wise! I shall cut off my red brush, my servant, and throw him away."

But All-Wise replied:

"First let your red brush tell us why he dragged on the ground."

And the fine red brush explained:

"Because I was heavy with water and mud from the river."

Then All-Wise the Dwarf asked further:

"And why were you heavy?"

And the fine red brush answered:

"Because Rufusi Ryneker did not shake me enough when he came out of the river, and he came ashore in a very muddy place."

Then All-Wise the Dwarf said:

"Think again, Rufusi Ryneker. Whose fault was it really that the hounds almost caught you today?"

And Rufusi Ryneker confessed humbly:

"It was not my red brush's fault; it was my own. You are right,

All-Wise; I am not wise, I'm just clever. How did you know? And how can I learn to be wise?"

And All-Wise the Dwarf replied:

"I knew because you did not say 'thank you' when you came in through my green door. Learn to be grateful, Rufusi Ryneker, to your servants who serve you so faithfully, and to the stones on which you tread, and to the plants which shelter you, and to the air you breathe, and to the sun which gives you light. That is how you will grow to be wise. And one day you will come again on some forest path to the little House of Crowning, and I will hold its green door open, and I will say, 'come in, Rufusi Ryneker,' and I will crown you with the crown of candles, and the gems in the hearts of their flames will light up your head."

Then All-Wise the Dwarf stamped three times, and said to the House of Crowning:

"Up, little house,
To sun and air!
Up, little house,
To the forest fair!"

And immediately the House of Crowning rose above the ground, and All-Wise the Dwarf opened the little green door, and Rufusi Ryneker saw that they were in the middle of the forest path again, and the hounds and the huntsmen had gone, and night had fallen, and the stars were shining.

As Rufusi Ryneker said thank you and farewell to All-Wise the Dwarf and made his way home through the night, he began to feel quite differently towards his four Feet, and his two Eyes, and his two Ears, and his red Brush, who served him so quietly and faithfully, and to the trees which sheltered him, and to the stars which lit the darkness, and to the stones which made earth firm beneath his feet.

And at the memory of the crown of candles hanging in the little House of Crowning, and at the hope that All-Wise would one day crown him with it and that the gems at the hearts of the flames of the candles would light up his head, Rufusi Ryneker's heart was filled with joy, and with joy, and with great joy.

The Poem of the Crown of Candles

When the story was finished, Sylvia helped her mother to prepare the Advent apples. They chose the four rosiest, and cut out the core. In each apple, in the hole where the core had been, they put a coloured candle. And when teatime came, they put an Advent apple at each corner of the table, and lit the coloured candles, and had their meal by candlelight. And as the gentle glow and the gentle shadows fell on the Christmas roses in the middle of the table, and on the bowl of apples and oranges, and on Sylvia's mother's face, Sylvia thought they made everything lovelier.

Sylvia took one of the candles in its apple candlestick with her when she went to bed, and it turned the open page of her Wonder Book golden as she softly chanted her poetry spell:

> "Rhyme-elves, rich in ringing words
> Won from winds and waves and birds,
> Lisping leaves and rustling rain,
> Sing – sing – for me again!"

And the next morning, on the new page, there was a fine portrait of Rufusi Ryneker and his fine red brush for her to enjoy. When she took the Wonder Book into her mother's bed, this was the new poem her mother read to her:

Rufusi, Rufusi Ryneker,
Clever you are!
But when have you paused to be grateful
To stone or to star;
To air or to sun or to water,
To scent or to snow,
To all things and creatures that save you
    and serve you,
Above and below?

Rufusi, Rufusi Ryneker,
Thus will you grow wise;
And then will you find in the forest
The crown of the skies;
And when to the House of your Crowning
You one day are led,
The gems at the hearts of the flames of the
    candles
Shall light up your head.

The Visit of St Nicholas

A few days later, Sylvia had a St Nicholas Eve party; and she invited her six little friends to it – Joan and Terry and Rosaleen and Margaret and Stephen and Luke.

The old woodsman had said to Sylvia that morning:

"You know, tonight's the night when St Nicholas goes about the world, visiting little children. I wonder whether he will visit you?"

Sylvia told Joan and Terry and Rosaleen and Margaret and Stephen and Luke what the old woodsman had said so when there suddenly came three loud knocks at the door in the middle of "hunt the slipper," they all became as still as mice, and everyone was thinking:

"I wonder if that's St Nicholas?"

Then Sylvia's mother said quietly:

"Open the door, Sylvia, and see who is there!"

So Sylvia got up and went to the door; and her heart was going *thump – thump – thump*. She opened the door; and there stood St Nicholas.

And St Nicholas asked:

"May I come in, Sylvia?"

Sylvia opened the door wider, and St Nicholas came in, wearing a magnificent red cloak, with his golden bishop's hat on his head, and with his golden bishop's crook in his hand, and under his arm he carried an enormous golden book.

Behind him Rupert, his little page boy, came skipping in

with a stick in one hand, and a birch twig broom in the other, a bulging sack over one shoulder, and a twinkle in both eyes.

All the children still sat like mice in their circle on the carpet, and stared and stared and stared. But Sylvia's mother welcomed St Nicholas, and offered him a chair; and St Nicholas thanked her and sat down, with Rupert standing beside him.

Then St Nicholas looked around at all the children, and said:

"In this big golden book of mine are the names of all the children everywhere in the world; and their good deeds are written on the golden pages, and their bad deeds on the black ones."

And he opened the book at a black page and read out some of their bad deeds. But no-one felt hurt or told off when he read out their faults because before they could feel bad, Rupert the little page boy landed in front of each child with a hop, skip and a jump and with a twinkle in both eyes, and out of his bulging sack came some lovely gift to help them overcome each fault. Sylvia's was a box of the most beautiful velvet hair ribbons she had ever seen, to help her to stop getting her curls all tangled up. She thought it was as if Rupert had been peeping into her wardrobe because there was a velvet ribbon to match every dress she had.

Then St Nicholas turned to a golden page, and told Rupert to reward the children for all their good deeds; so Rupert opened his sack again, and brought out the best gifts each of children could have asked for. To Sylvia, Rupert gave a set of little biscuit cutters shaped like stars and hearts and crescent moons and flowers and tiny trees – exactly what she wanted for cutting out biscuits for Christmas and her birthday.

Then Rupert chased all the children around the room, their shrieks of laughter getting louder and louder. When they were tired he lent the children his birch twig broom and they took turns sweeping up the silver paper and coloured wools and other things from the party till the room was tidy again. Finally Rupert took out apples and nuts and sweets from his sack, and gave some to all the children.

Then St Nicholas said goodbye and went out again into the starlit night, with Rupert skipping behind him and waving his empty sack and his stick and his birch twig broom. When they were gone Sylvia and Joan and Terry and Rosaleen and Margaret and Stephen and Luke all sat down on the carpet again in a circle, and hugged their gifts, and talked about St Nicholas. They all laughed at the funny things Rupert had given them to help overcome their faults and agreed that he was a very funny boy.

And then Sylvia begged:

"Mother, please tell us a story about St Nicholas!"

And Joan and Terry and Rosaleen and Margaret and Stephen and Luke all cried:

"Oh yes, please, tell us a story about St Nicholas!"

So they put out the big lights, and lit two of the candles on the Advent wreath, and sat in a circle in the firelight while Sylvia's mother told them the story of Bella, Sophia and little Bonita.

And this is it:

The Story of Bella, Sophia and Little Bonita

One December, long, long ago, St Nicholas and his page boy, Rupert, were travelling around the world, St Nicholas with his golden crook and his golden book, and Rupert with his big stick, and his birch twig broom, and his bulging sack over his shoulder, and a twinkle in both eyes. And on a starlit night when snow was on the ground, they came to the Valley of the Sleeping Dragon.

When Rupert heard the dragon breathing in his sleep, his eyes stopped twinkling, and he stopped playing around, and he said fearfully to St Nicholas:

"Good master, *must* we go through this valley? What if we wake up the dragon?"

St Nicholas reassured him:

"We must go through this valley, Rupert; for it leads to the Plain of the Black Morass, where there are children who would be sad if we did not visit them. But have no fear; this dragon eats only golden boys, and nothing wakes him except a golden boy being born."

So Rupert went up on his tiptoes, held on to his big stick very tightly in case the dragon awoke by mistake and kept very close to St Nicholas as they walked. After a while they passed safely through the Valley of the Sleeping Dragon and arrived at the Plain of the Black Morass. And right in front of them they could see the lights of a village shining; and outside the village was a half-ruined stable. As they came closer to the stable, they could smell peat smoke and see firelight flickering through the holes in its tumble-down walls.

Rupert's eyes twinkled in amazement, and he asked:

"Surely, no one lives in this tumble-down stable, good master?"

And St Nicholas replied:

"Yes, an old sick father, who is very poor, lives there with three young daughters, Bella the beautiful, Sophia the wise, and Bonita, who is little and good."

Then Rupert asked:

"What do you need from my sack, good master, to help Bella, Sophia and little Bonita to overcome their faults?"

Standing in the snow and the starlight, St Nicholas opened his big golden book, and turned over its black pages; but he could not see the names of Bella, Sophia and little Bonita light up anywhere. Then he turned to the golden pages, and their names lit up, and he read out to Rupert:

"Bella had an enchanted cow, her most treasured possession; and she sold it to buy bread for her sick father. Sophia had a spinning wheel, her most treasured possession; and she sold it to buy bread for her sick father. Little Bonita had a sturdy donkey, her most treasured possession; and she sold it to buy bread for her sick father."

Then Rupert gave a hop, a skip and a jump, and asked:

"What gifts do you need from my sack, to reward Bella, Sophia and little Bonita, good master?"

And St Nicholas replied:

"Lets find out what they would like best."

So St Nicholas and Rupert stood quietly in the snow and the starlight outside the stable, and looked in through a hole in the wall. And they saw the peat fire smouldering on the stable floor; and beside it, on a bed of straw, the old sick father was lying; and around it, on three tree stumps, sat Bella, Sophia and little Bonita, drying a long piece of fine white linen.

And St Nicholas and Rupert heard Sophia say:

"This is my last piece, dear sisters. Tomorrow we must sell it to buy bread. And after that, we have nothing left in all the world that we can sell."

Then Bella sighed, and gazed upwards, and said:

"The sky is so full of gold tonight – crowded with stars looking down through the holes in our roof. If only it would spare us a little!"

And little Bonita gazed upwards, too, and said dreamily:

"Yes, if only we had just three little pieces of gold we would be happy. We could buy back Bella's enchanted cow to give us milk again, and Sophia's spinning wheel to spin for us again, and my sturdy donkey to fetch peat from the black morass to keep our fire burning again."

And Bella and Sophia cried together:

"Ah, little Bonita, what a wonderful gift that would be!"

Then St Nicholas, listening outside in the snow and the starlight, whispered to Rupert:

"Rupert, quietly give me the gifts they long for."

So with a hop Rupert set down his sack in the snow, and with a skip he opened it, and with a jump he took out three golden coins and gave them to St Nicholas. And St Nicholas gently tossed them through the hole in the wall; and with a *clink, clink, clink,* they fell on the hearthstone at the feet of Bella, Sophia and little Bonita.

Bella, Sophia and little Bonita wondered what strange gifts had appeared in their home. When they saw what they had been given, they joyfully showed the golden coins to their father, and then ran to the door, to thank whoever had thrown them. But St Nicholas and Rupert had disappeared, on their way to bring joy and gifts to other children in the village; and Bella, Sophia and little Bonita found there was no one there.

So they went happily together out into the snow and the starlight, each with her golden coin, to buy back Bella's enchanted cow and Sophia's spinning wheel and little Bonita's sturdy donkey.

And when they had returned, each with her most treasured possession, and the stable was filled with their gratitude and joy, there came a sudden knock at the door; and little Bonita ran and opened it. And outside stood an old bearded man in a tattered cloak, and beside him a lady, who seemed sick with tiredness.

The old man asked humbly:

"Could we beg for shelter for the night, kind people? The lady is so weary, she can go no further."

Then the old sick father called from his bed of straw:

"Come in and welcome, travellers!"

And they came in thankfully.

Then Sophia made the lady a bed on the straw; and Bella milked her enchanted cow, and brought milk to the lady and the old man; and little Bonita took her sturdy donkey through the snow and the starlight to the black morass for peat to feed the fire to keep the lady and the old man warm.

And that night a golden boy was born in the stable.

Then little Bonita heated water on the peat fire, and washed the golden boy. And Bella brought milk from her enchanted cow, and gave the golden boy his first earthly food. And Sophia took her last piece of fine linen, which they had been going to sell next day, and made swaddling clothes for the golden boy. And when they took back the golden boy, washed, fed and clothed, to lay him in the lady's arms, they saw she had a sun beaming upon her heart, and a coronet of stars shining upon her hair, and around her waist she wore a silver belt, with silver fringes reaching to her knees.

And as they gazed in joy and amazement at the sight of the lady and the golden child, a new noise broke the silence, like rumbling thunder very far away.

And Bella exclaimed:

"Listen – the dragon is stirring in his sleep! He will wake up as soon as the sun comes up and then he try to harm the golden boy. Sophia, Bonita, we must think quickly. How can we save the golden boy?"

And Sophia replied:

"The golden boy will be safe on the other side of the black morass far away from the dragon. But he must be there by sunrise."

But their old sick father said in distress:

"No one can make their way across the black morass by night. One false step and the deep bog would swallow them."

And little Bonita answered cheerily:

"My sturdy donkey can find the way, he has been there so many times to fetch peat to feed our fire."

So Bella gave the old man milk and their last bread for the journey; and Sophia took what was left of her last piece of fine linen, and wrapped it like a white cloak around the golden boy. The lady thanked them, and sat upon little Bonita's sturdy donkey, wrapping the golden boy in the shelter of her arms and warming him with the sun that beamed upon her heart. With the old man trudging alongside, she rode slowly away across the black morass through the snow and the starlight, while far away in his valley, like a distant thunderstorm, the dragon stirred in his sleep.

Bella, Sophia and little Bonita stood at the open door until they couldn't see the lady's coronet of stars any longer. And when they came back into the stable, their father cried in amazement:

"Bella, Bella! What is beaming on your heart?"

And when Sophia and little Bonita looked at Bella, they saw that, like the mother of the golden boy, she had a sun beaming from her chest.

And again their father cried in amazement:

"Sophia, Sophia! What is shining on your hair?"

And when Bella and little Bonita looked at Sophia, they saw that, like the mother of the golden boy, she had a coronet of stars upon her head.

And yet again their father cried in amazement:

"Little Bonita, how your belt glitters!"

And when Bella and Sophia looked at little Bonita, they saw that, like the mother of the golden boy, she wore a silver belt, and its silver fringes reached from her waist to her knees.

Then little Bonita ran the silver fringes lovingly through her fingers, and cried happily:

"With these I can buy another sturdy donkey to fetch peat to feed the fire and keep us all warm."

But their father said:

"There is no longer any need, my little Bonita. See – I am able to work again myself, for my dear daughters!"

And he got up from his bed of straw; and they saw that he wasn't sick any more; he had been made strong and well.

And Bella, Sophia and little Bonita cheered, and ran to their father, and hugged him.

And the distant thunder ceased; and their father said:

"Listen! The dragon is fast asleep again. The golden boy must already be safe beyond the black morass."

Then together they drank all of the milk from the enchanted cow, and warmed themselves at the peat fire, and looked up thankfully through the holes in the roof at the sky so full of gold, and went happily to sleep.

The Poem of the Golden Boy

When Sylvia's mother had finished the story, the children sat silently, seeing lovely pictures in the fire. They saw the golden boy, and Bella with the sun beaming on her heart, and Sophia in her coronet of stars, and little Bonita with her long-fringed silver belt. Then there came three loud knocks at the door again, and Sylvia ran to open it.

This time it was the old woodsman, who had come with Blackbird and her cart to take Joan and Terry and Rosaleen and Margaret and Stephen and Luke home.

So they all hurried about, laughing and talking about St Nicholas and Rupert while Joan and Terry and Rosaleen and Margaret and Stephen and Luke got their shoes and coats on.

Then Joan and Terry and Rosaleen and Margaret and Stephen and Luke collected all their gifts; and said goodbye to Sylvia and her mother, telling them that it was the most wonderful party they had ever been to. Then they all streamed out into the starlight, and the old woodsman lifted them one by one on to the soft hay inside the cart, and tucked them in with warm rugs, laughing his slow, cosy laugh

Then everyone shouted goodnight again; and off went Blackbird, her cart rumbling behind her, her hoofs going *clip – clop – clop*. Soon the little bursts of laughter from the children grew fainter, and the lantern swinging behind the cart grew smaller till it was as little as a star.

Then Sylvia and her mother went indoors again; and Sylvia felt suddenly so sleepy that she could barely keep awake long enough to undress and tumble into bed and put her Wonder Book on the bedside table beside Rupert's gifts, and softly chant her poetry spell:

> "Rhyme-elves, rich in ringing words
> Won from winds and waves and birds,
> Lisping leaves and rustling rain,
> Sing – sing – for me again!"

It seemed only a moment before it was morning and Sylvia was awake again. She gazed happily at the Wonder Book's new picture of St Nicholas and Rupert in the snow outside the stable. And when she took her Wonder Book into her mother's bed, this was the new poem her mother read to her:

> Dream – dream –
> Bella's enchanted cow!
> Give her your milk with joy;
> The hour is nearing now
> When she a golden boy
> Gently to earth shall bring
> Through your sweet caring.
> Where his bright head has pressed,
> A sun beams from her chest.
> Dream – dream –
> Bella's enchanted cow!
>
> Whirl – whirl –
> Sophia's spinning wheel!
> Beneath her careful hands

The flax-thread fills the reel,
To weave soft swaddling bands
A golden boy to wrap,
Alight upon her lap.
Now on her hair be set
Stars in a coronet.
Whirl – whirl –
Sophia's spinning wheel!

Plod – plod –
Bonita's sturdy donkey!
Beyond the black morass
Where the dragon doesn't see
A golden boy you bear.
Bonita bids you go
Steadfastly through the snow.
Now shall her belt be
Silver from waist to knee.
Plod – plod –
Bonita's sturdy donkey!

Sylvia's Painting

A few days later, the old woodsman came with Blackbird to take Sylvia's mother to do her Christmas shopping. While her mother was getting ready, Sylvia ran out with a carrot for Blackbird, and asked the old woodsman:

"Please, Mr Woodsman, what do you think my mother would like me to get her for Christmas?"

The old woodsman thought for a moment; then he said:

"I think she might like you to paint her a picture."

Sylvia thought for a moment, too; then she asked:

"Do you think she would like a picture of the first Christmas?"

And the old woodsman smiled and said:

"I'm sure she would!"

So as soon as Blackbird and the old woodsman had gone *clip-clop-clopping* away, taking Sylvia's mother with them, Sylvia ran back into the white cottage. She got out a big sheet of painting paper and her sponge and her brushes and a mug of water and the little glass jars of paint her mother mixed for her.

And first she dampened the paper all over with her sponge, to make the paint flow softly; and then she dipped her brush in the jar of heavenly blue, and began to paint the sky.

Next she painted the bright green grass below it, and then the crib with a gentle yellow light around it. She painted Mary sitting near the crib in her blue cloak, and on one side the three kings standing in purple robes and enormous crowns. On the other side she painted the shepherds in their brown jackets running down the hillside and waving their arms and falling over their crooks in their excitement.

Sylvia washed her brush carefully each time before she dipped it in a jar of paint, just as her mother had taught her, so that the colours wouldn't get mixed up. Sylvia was so absorbed in painting that time flew by until she suddenly heard the *clip – clop – clop* of Blackbird returning. She jumped up to put away the picture quickly before her mother came in; and her hand knocked over the mug of water spilling it right across the picture. The sky and grass and crib and kings and shepherds all began to drown before her eyes.

Sylvia sobbed and sobbed, desperately trying to mop up the flood with her sponge, but before she knew it her mother's arm was about her, and she was saying comfortingly:

"There, there! We'll just brush the water away here, and make the sky a little bluer there, and put the green back into the grass, and look – it's nearly right again already!"

As she spoke her other hand was busy with the paint brush, saving Sylvia's picture.

Then Sylvia dried her tears, and blew hard into her handkerchief, and said:

"Oh, I just wanted it to be beautiful for you!"

And her mother replied cheerfully:

"And it is. You know, Sylvia, whenever you try hard and it doesn't turn out quite right, it helps if you remember what the lily said to the fir tree."

Sensing another story Sylvia completely forgot to cry and asked eagerly:

"Oh, Mother, what did the lily say? Is it a story?"

So Sylvia's mother took off her outdoor things and sat down by the big log fire. Sylvia sat on her mother's knee and leaned against her shoulder with her arm warm and strong and comforting about her. And while Sylvia watched the flames leaping, only sniffling a little now and then, her mother told her the story of the tree that dreamt a flower.

And this is it:

The Story of the Tree that Dreamt a Flower

There was once an archer, who lived among the stars, and whose arrows were not meant to wound but to bring love for all things good and beautiful.

One day he shot an arrow which fell to Earth on a cold and naked mountainside, where no plant had ever grown. And the arrow's feathers turned into roots, and the arrow grew into a tree. And this tree was the first fir tree.

The tree grew straight and tall, pointing to the stars. And as the tree looked up at the stars, she loved them, because they were good and beautiful. So every day she grew taller, because she longed to reach them.

Now the stones of that desolate place had been very happy when the green fir tree came to live with them; but when they saw her always reaching towards the stars, they were afraid that she would grow right away from them.

So the stones cried out to her:

"Do not forget us altogether, dear fir tree. It is alright for you to love the stars; but please love Earth a little, too."

The fir tree listened, and looked down, and felt sorry for the stones who were stuck in the ground, and she sent her roots down deeper to embrace them. And she began to love the stones and the soil a little, as well as the sky and the stars.

Then the small creatures who lived on that cold and naked mountainside, and who longed for shade and shelter, also cried out to the fir tree:

"Dear fir tree, do not forget us, either. We are glad that your head is lifted towards the stars; but will you not lower your arms a little towards Earth, to bring us shade and shelter?"

And the fir tree listened, and looked down, and felt sorry for the small creatures of the mountainside; and she let her branches droop until the lowest brushed the ground with their outstretched fingers. And the small creatures of the mountainside crept beneath the fir tree thankfully, and found shelter there from the storms, and warmth when the nights were cold.

And now, with her straight trunk, and her drooping branches, and her sharp tip pointing to the stars, the fir tree began to form the shape of the arrow she had once been.

And she grew to love Earth more and more, and to take more and more soil into her sap, until soon she was wrapped in bark, and her wood grew to be less and less soft like a plant, and more and more hard like a stone.

And now, where she had dropped her pine needle leaves to the ground, the bare soil became gradually richer, so that mosses, and small creeping plants, and eventually taller plants, began to cover the once empty mountainside. And water plants began to grow in the little mountain pools that were made where rain gathered between the rocks. And among these was a lily plant, which looked up in love and wonder at the fir tree, and listened with delight and longing when the fir tree spoke of the stars to the stones and the small creatures nestling beneath her branches.

To them it was all like a wonderful fairy story; for the stones, stuck in the ground, couldn't see the sky; and the animals, who moved on four legs, couldn't lift their heads high enough to gaze upwards at the stars. And the mosses and the stones and the small creatures and the lily plant would sigh:

"Oh, if only a star would come down and live among us!"

Now the fir tree often wondered how this might be possible, for she wanted the stones and the mosses and the small creatures of the mountainside to be able to share her own joy in the goodness and the beauty of the stars. Then one night she had a dream.

In this dream she said a powerful magic spell, which called a star down to Earth. And a star came curving like a falling spark out of the sky, and entered her roots. And eventually the star broke out through the bark of one of her branches, wrapped inside a bud. Then the bud opened and became a gorgeous flower with delicate petals. And that flower was the most beautiful thing that had ever existed on the Earth.

Now this story happened long, long ago, when the Earth was still very young, and there had never been any flowers at all before; so the fir tree's dream was the first dream of the first flower.

And the lily plant, looking up in love and wonder at the fir tree, saw the wonderful pictures of the fir tree's dream painted on the air about her.

Now when the fir tree woke up, she remembered her dream; and she also remembered the magic spell she had spoken in her dream. And she said to herself:

"Is this really the way to bring a star to brighten up the Earth? Can I make my dream come true?"

So she said the magic spell of her dream; a powerful spell to call a star down to Earth. And the lily plant, looking up to her in love and wonder, heard her speak the magic spell.

And, just as in her dream, a star came curving like a falling spark out of the sky, and entered the fir tree's roots. And eventually, again as in her dream, the star broke out through the bark of one of her branches, wrapped inside a bud. And the fir tree trembled with happiness; and the lily plant, looking up to the fir tree in love and wonder, trembled with happiness with her.

But what happened next was different from the dream. For the strength and stiffness of the fir tree's wood entered into the bud, so that it became woody, too. The bud sat on her branch like

a stone, the colour of a stone; and when it opened, it wasn't the gorgeous flower she had dreamed of. Instead of delicate petals it had thick, hard scales. It was not a real flower; it was a fir cone.

And the fir tree cried in distress:

"I can never make my beautiful dream come true! There is too much soil in my sap."

And she was so sad at her failure that she began to weep. But through her weeping she heard a sweet voice, speaking words of comfort to her from below. And when she looked down, she saw that it was the lily plant that grew in the mountain pool the rain had made between the rocks.

And the lily plant said:

"Do not weep, dear fir tree, for you have done a new and a wonderful thing. You have taught the stars how to become flowers; and with your permission I, and other tender plants, can still make your dream come true."

And the fir tree dried her tears, and answered:

"With all my heart."

So the lily plant spoke aloud the magic spell, which she had learnt from the fir tree, to call a star down to Earth. And a star came curving like a falling spark out of the sky, and entered the lily plant's roots.

Now there was no soil in the lily-plant's roots as she lived with her feet in water, and every part of her was soft and delicate and tender. Soon a stem grew up from between her leaves, and on the stem there was a soft bud and inside the bud was the star. The bud opened and out came a gorgeous flower with delicate petals, just as beautiful as the flower in the fir tree's dream. This was the first real flower and it was a lily. And because a six-pointed star had entered the lily plant's roots, the lily had six petals too.

And just like the lily plant, in love and in wonder, had learnt how to call stars down from the sky and turn them into flowers from the fir tree, all the other tender plants learnt from the lily plant.

And the fir tree was overjoyed to see her dream come true.

And the flower of the lily plant told her:

"I heard a prophecy among the stars, dear fir tree, while I was still a star myself before I came to Earth. And this was it: because you were the first plant to long to bring a star to Earth and give birth to a flower, and because you longed to give this beautiful gift to the stones and the small creatures, the time will come when once every year you will be covered from tip to toe with stars and flowers and gifts and covered with candles. And just as the small mountain creatures love you now, so little children everywhere will love you. You will be the most beautiful and best-loved tree in all the world!"

And that is how the archer's arrow became the Christmas tree.

The Poem of the Christmas Tree

After the story of the tree that dreamt a flower, Sylvia felt much better so she went back to her painting and realised that the picture wasn't spoilt after all; in fact it was more beautiful than before.

Sylvia took Titania to bed with her that night, to remind her of the story, because Titania had once been a Christmas tree fairy. She put out her Wonder Book, open at a new page, and softly chanted her poetry spell:

> "Rhyme-elves, rich in ringing words
> Won from winds and waves and birds,
> Lisping leaves and rustling rain,
> Sing – sing – for me again!"

When she woke up the next morning, there on the new page was a new picture of the fir tree growing on the naked mountainside. And when she and Titania took the Wonder Book into her mother's bed, this was the new poem her mother read to them:

> The Christmas tree
> Sets in the crystal snow
> The warmth of candle glow.
>
> The Christmas tree
> In winter's shivering gloom
> Makes fire-red roses bloom.
>
> The Christmas tree
> Be-diamonds with its light
> December's darkest night.
>
> The Christmas tree
> In the sun's feeblest hour
> Brings barren branches to flower.
>
> The Christmas tree
> For all this waiting Earth
> Brings Christmas stars to birth.
>
> Star, rose and candle be
> Gifts on each Christmas tree!

Getting Ready for Christmas

When Sylvia's mother had read the poem of the Christmas Tree to Sylvia and Titania, she asked:

"Would you like us to go and see the old woodsman today, Sylvia, and choose your Christmas tree?"

Sylvia was so excited that she jumped with joy and soon after breakfast she and her mother set off along the woodland path to visit the old woodsman. Before long they saw him at work among his trees; and Sylvia ran towards him, throwing her arms around his legs. He showed them round his nursery of young fir trees but Sylvia found it very difficult to choose her Christmas tree. She would have liked them all to have the joy of being covered from tip to toe with stars and roses and gifts and lighted candles.

And the old woodsman said:

"Of course each fir tree hopes it will be the one you choose, because every fir tree longs to go inside a house and share Christmas with a child. But don't worry because even those that stay out in the starlight will have their Christmas too, with the snow to cover them and the wind to tell them stories."

This made Sylvia feel much happier so she chose one which was just her height and the old woodsman promised to bring it to the white cottage on Christmas Eve. He said that he would dig it up carefully and not hurt its roots, so that when Christmas was over, Sylvia could plant it in her garden beside the fairy tree.

Sylvia counted the days until Christmas Eve but they sped by so quickly, because she had to do so much to get ready for Christmas! There were all the presents to finish making, and to wrap in coloured paper and tie with coloured ribbon. She needed presents for her mother and the old woodsman and Joan and Terry and Rosaleen and Margaret and Luke and Stephen. There were biscuits to be cut into trees and stars and flowers and hearts and crescent moons using the cutters St Nicholas had given her. There were mince pies to make; and the Christmas pudding and the Christmas cake and Sylvia's birthday cake, as well, to be mixed and stirred and baked and iced. And there were moon and star candleholders to be made out of acorn-cups and beech-nut cups, and gilded with gold paint; and baskets to hold rainbow-coloured sweets to be made out of gold paper.

And every evening, after all this busyness, she enjoyed quiet time sitting in the firelight with her mother, practising carols while the candles on the Advent wreath – first three, then all four of them – shone softly in the darkness.

At last it was Christmas Eve and after lunch the old woodsman arrived, with a cluster of holly berries in his hat and another on Blackbird's bridle. He brought Sylvia's fir tree and a big armful of holly and a little bunch of the mistletoe which grew on his old apple tree. And when he had carried the tree tub into a corner of the living room and put soil into it, he and Sylvia and her mother planted the Christmas tree in it together.

After the old woodsman and Blackbird had gone on to the village, with Blackbird's cart full of holly and mistletoe and Christmas trees for Joan and Terry and Rosaleen and Margaret and Stephen and Luke, Sylvia and her mother put holly all around the room; and then came the lovely, lovely task of decorating the Christmas tree.

There were thirty-three red roses and thirty-three white candles to fasten on its branches, and golden stars and golden sweet baskets and apples and oranges. Then there were all the gifts in their coloured wrappings to pile on the floor below. And last of all, Sylvia laid silver lengths of frosty tinsel over all the branches.

By the time they were finished it was nearly dark, so Sylvia's mother lit the four candles on the Advent wreath, then gave Sylvia the taper. Holding her breath, Sylvia very, very carefully lit all thirty-three white candles on the Christmas tree, one-by-one.

And when she stood back to look at it, shining and shimmering and glimmering and glittering in the candle light, it was so beautiful that she couldn't stopping staring. Everything on the tree shone softly with gentle lights and colours and gleams of gold and silver; it was so beautiful. Sylvia sat down on the rug in front of the fire, leaned against her mother's knee, and stared and stared at the tree.

After a moment she murmured:

"I wonder if there's ever been anyone as beautiful as a Christmas tree?"

And her mother smiled and answered:

"I think kind Cordita must have been!"

And Sylvia begged:

"Oh, Mother, please tell me about her!"

So, sitting in the firelight and the candle light, with the tree shining so beautifully, her mother told her this story, the story of Cordita and the three little men:

The Story of Cordita and the Three Little Men

There was once a king who had one son who he loved dearly. When this prince was born, his fairy godmothers gathered round his cradle, and each gave him a gift. One said he would be handsome; one said he would be good; one said he would marry the kindest maiden in the kingdom; one said that summer's golden bird would fly about this maiden's head; and one said that a shower of gems would fall from her lips every time she spoke.

And when all except the last of the fairy godmothers had spoken, a wicked fairy appeared beside the cradle; and she cried triumphantly:

"In spite of all your promises, the prince shall be deceived, and shall marry the wrong maiden."

Then the king turned in horror to the last fairy godmother, and begged her:

"Can you not lift this curse from my beloved child?"

And the last fairy godmother answered:

"I cannot destroy the curse entirely; but I will give the prince this gift so that he can protect himself from its danger – that in silence he shall find wisdom."

The years passed, and when the young prince was old enough to be married the king sent a message throughout his kingdom that if anyone found a maiden who had summer's golden bird flying about her head and from whose lips fell a shower of gems each time she spoke, they were to send word at once to the royal palace. But the weeks went by, and the months went by, and there was no news.

Now living on the other side of the mountains from the royal palace there lived a beautiful maiden named Cordita. She didn't have anyone in the world except for her cruel stepmother and her ugly stepsister, who was called Kapala. They made Cordita work hard all day in the kitchen, and gave her nothing but rags to wear. All she was given to eat was a dry crust of bread in the evening, and at night they made her sleep in the loft over the stable. But Cordita was so gentle that she put up with it all and never complained.

One terribly cold winter's night Cordita was trudging wearily across the courtyard to her bed in the stable, carrying her crust of bread in one hand and a lantern in the other, when suddenly she heard three faint, whimpering calls for help. She was so kind-hearted that even though the icy wind was blowing through her thin rags and she had to walk through the snow in her bare feet, she had to search for whoever had called out for help. At last, beside the well in the middle of the courtyard, she found three little men imprisoned in a block of ice, where they were slowly freezing to death.

Cordita couldn't believe her eyes and cried out:

"Oh, you poor little men! Just wait while I find a stone to break the ice!"

And she dug in the deep snow with her hands until she found a stone. But though she hammered the block of ice as hard as she could, it wouldn't break.

Then the first little man called out to her through the ice:

"Kind Cordita, the ice would melt if you lit a fire beside it. Do you think you could do that?"

And kind Cordita answered:

"I will do that gladly."

And she broke off twigs from the bare branches of the lime tree which grew over the well; and she opened her lantern and took out the candle inside and tried to light the twigs with it. But the twigs would not catch fire.

Then the second little man called out to her through the ice:

"Kind Cordita, the fire could be kindled by a drop of blood given by a maiden out of her own heart. Do you think you could do that?"

And kind Cordita answered:

"I will do that gladly."

And she arranged the twigs across the candle, and opened the rags covering her chest, and pricked herself with a pin so that a drop of blood fell down on to the twigs. All at once a bright red flame shot up. The twigs began to burn, and the ice began to melt, and – hey presto! – there stood the three little men, released from their imprisonment.

All three men thanked her and then the third little man asked:

"Kind Cordita, we are hungry. Could you spare us a little bread?"

And kind Cordita answered:

"I will do that gladly. Come with me into the stable where you will be sheltered."

And she opened the stable door and led them in, and set down her lantern, and they all sat round it. Cordita broke her crust of bread into four pieces, and she and the three little men ate her day's food together.

And when they had finished eating, the first little man said:

"To reward Cordita for her kindness, I will give her a gift. As soon as the sun rises tomorrow, summer's golden bird shall fly about her head."

And the second little man said:

"To reward Cordita for her kindness, I too will give her a gift. A shower of gems shall fall from her lips each time she speaks, starting from the first time she answers a question."

And the third little man said:

"To reward Cordita for her kindness, I will give her a gift as well. When a white horse has spent three nights in this stable, a king's son shall make her his bride."

Cordita thanked them shyly but the very next moment, all three little men had vanished.

When Cordita came out of the stable next morning to begin her long day's work, the sun was just rising; and as its first ray touched her, summer's golden bird began to fly about her head. And with every step she took, the snow melted; and the harsh wind grew soft and warm; and the whole courtyard was filled with flowers. The lime tree over the well was covered with blossom with bees humming in the blossom, and the bare bushes in the corners of the courtyard grew new green leaves, and from their branches birds began to sing.

The bird song was so loud and joyful that it could be heard throughout the house and it woke Kapala up. Hearing the noise she got out of bed and went to the window to see what was the matter. In the courtyard below her window she saw the blossoming lime tree, with Cordita standing underneath the tree drawing water from the well and there was a golden bird flying about her head.

As soon as she saw it, Kapala wanted the golden bird for herself: how dare Cordita own anything so beautiful! So she ran into her mother's room, where she was sleeping, shook her awake, and shouted:

"Mother, Cordita has a wonderful golden bird. Take it away from her and give it to me!"

Her mother got out of bed and went to the window, and stood amazed at the bird song and the humming of the bees and the melting of the snow and the warm wind and the blossoming lime tree and the courtyard full of flowers. And when she saw Cordita drawing water from the well with summer's golden bird flying about her head, she dressed quickly and went down into the courtyard, and asked Cordita sharply:

"Cordita, where did that golden bird come from?"

And Cordita answered modestly:

"There were three little men in the courtyard last night, Stepmother, and the golden bird was a gift from one of them."

And as she spoke, a shower of gems fell from her lips.

Her stepmother stared at the gems sparkling among the flowers, and greedily gathered them up, and sharply asked again:

"And who gave you *this* gift, Cordita?"

And again Cordita answered modestly:

"Another of the little men, Stepmother."

And again a shower of gems fell from her lips.

And when the stepmother had greedily gathered those as well, she asked again:

"And what gift did the third one give you?"

108

Cordita blushed and answered shyly:

"He promised that a king's son would make me his bride."

And again a shower of gems fell from her lips.

As soon as the stepmother heard this, she said to herself as she gathered those gems too:

"How can I make the king's son marry Kapala instead?"

She began to devise a plan.

But first she grabbed the golden bird roughly with two hands, and called Kapala to hold him tightly while she tied a strong cord about his leg. She fastened the other end of the cord firmly to a lock of Kapala's hair. Then she waited and every time that Cordita spoke, her stepmother greedily gathered up the shower of gems which fell from her lips, and put them in a great iron chest.

Then she ordered a messenger with a swift horse to ride across the snowy mountain to the royal palace. When he was brought into the king's presence, he knelt and gave this message:

"O King, my mistress bids me to tell you that though snow lies deep everywhere else in your kingdom, in her courtyard it is summer; and summer's golden bird flies round her daughter's head; and from her daughter's lips falls a shower of gems each time she speaks."

The king asked the messenger whether this was really true and the messenger replied:

"O King, with my own eyes I have seen the lime tree blossoming in the courtyard, and the golden bird flying about the maiden's head; and my mistress has shown me a great iron chest filled with the gems that have fallen from her daughter's lips."

Then the king was filled with joy but he had not forgotten the wicked fairy's curse. So he sent the messenger back on his swift horse with this message:

"The king's son himself will come to spend three days with this maiden. And if at the end of three days he is happy then he will bring her back to the royal palace and make her his bride."

And he called his son to him, and said:

"My son, get ready to go and spend three days with this maiden. I send you alone, for only your own heart can tell whether this is your godmother's choice or the fairy curse at work. But take these three gifts; give the golden shoes to her after the first night, and the golden comb after the second; they will help you to decide whether she is the false bride or the real one. And if your heart is content after the third night, give her the golden dress, but if your heart is not content, remember your godmother's promise that you will find wisdom in silence."

Then the king's son took the three gifts, embraced his father, saddled his white horse, and set off alone across the snowy mountain.

Meanwhile the messenger had returned to the stepmother, and given her the king's message. And her evil heart rejoiced. She dressed Kapala in her richest garments but warned her:

"Make sure that you do not speak a single word to the king's son. You have only to be careful for three days, and you will be a princess for the rest of your life."

And to Cordita the stepmother said:

"Keep out of sight while the king's son is here. You are never to leave the kitchen except to go to your stable at night."

So Cordita did not see the king's son arrive, riding his white horse.

As he entered the courtyard he saw that it was filled with flowers though the snow still lay deep around, and that the lime tree covered with blossom. He heard the singing of the birds and the humming of the bees, and felt the soft warm wind, his heart beat quickly in his chest in excitement. He said to himself:

"Surely I will find the bride my godmothers chose here!"

But when the stepmother met him and brought him into the house and presented Kapala to him, he was confused. He had thought his bride would be beautiful but Kapala was quite ugly and the golden bird was not flying happily round her head, as he had expected, but was beating its wings as if it was trying to escape. And he wondered to himself:

"Could this strange looking girl really be the kindest maiden in my father's kingdom?"

But he greeted her politely and when she curtsied but did not speak to him in return, her mother quickly explained:

"Your Royal Highness, my daughter is so overcome with joy at your arrival that it has temporarily robbed her of her voice. But come with me and I will show you the gems which fall from her lips when she speaks."

And she opened the great iron chest, and showed him the gems which had fallen from Cordita's lips.

And the king's son was more confused than ever but he remembered that he would find wisdom in silence, so he said nothing about what he was thinking but graciously took his place at the feast Cordita had worked hard all day preparing for him.

After that long day's work Cordita was very weary that night as she trudged across the courtyard to her bed in the stable, her crust of bread in one hand and her lantern in the other. But when she opened the stable door, suddenly she was no longer tired because the light of her lantern fell on a magnificent white horse. She ran forward happily, and hung the lantern on a nail above his stall, and laid her cheek against his glossy neck, and murmured:

"Sleep tight tonight, beautiful white one! Three nights in the stable, and the king's son will make me his bride!"

And as she spoke, a shower of gems fell from her lips, and caught in the white horse's mane leaving it sparkling.

Then Cordita shared her crust of bread with the white horse, took her lantern from the nail, climbed up to her bed among the straw in the loft, and quickly went to sleep.

The next morning the king's son brought Kapala the golden shoes, as his father had instructed him to do. And they were so rich and expensive that Kapala grabbed them greedily, and quite forgetting her mother's warning, exclaimed:

"How fine I'll look in these!"

The king's son noticed that her voice had returned, and he watched for the shower of gems to fall from her lips; but there was no shower of gems. But he remembered that he would find wisdom in silence so once again he said nothing.

After breakfast he went to the stable to visit his white horse; and there, caught in the white horse's mane, a shower of gems was sparkling. Again he wondered, but still he said nothing and that night he left the feast early and hid himself in the shadows in the corner of the stable.

As he hid the door opened, and Cordita came in with her crust of bread in one hand and her lantern in the other. She hung the lantern on the nail above the white horse's stall, and as its light fell on her, it was clear how beautiful she was even though she was wearing rags. Again the king's son felt his heart beat quickly in his chest.

Cordita laid her cheek against the white horse's glossy neck, and murmured:

"Sleep tight tonight, beautiful white one! Two nights in the stable, and the king's son will make me his bride!"

And as she spoke, a shower of gems fell from her lips and were caught in the white horse's mane, leaving it sparkling.

Then again Cordita shared her crust of bread with the white horse, took her lantern from the nail, climbed up to her bed among the straw in the loft, and quickly went to sleep.

And the king's son watched her go and kept quiet.

The next morning the king's son gave Kapala the golden comb, as his father had instructed him to do. And it was so beautiful that she grabbed it greedily, and began at once to comb her hair with it. But before she realised what was happening, she had combed the knotted cord right off the lock of hair which her mother had tied it to, and freed the golden bird! With a chirp of joy it flew up, darted through the window, and flew out of sight. And still the king's son said nothing.

And that night again he left the feast early, and hid himself in the shadows in the corner of the stable. As he hid the door opened, and in came Cordita, with her crust of bread in one hand and her lantern in the other. And as she hung the lantern on the nail above the horse's stall, the king's son saw that the golden bird was flying happily about her head, with Kapala's loose cord still swinging from its leg.

And Cordita said to the golden bird:

"Come perch on my hand, beautiful golden one, so that I can free you from that cord."

And she held out her hand, and the golden bird perched on it. She set the bird down gently on the white horse's back, and freed its leg from the cord. And the shower of gems which had fallen from her lips were caught in the white horse's mane, leaving it sparkling.

Cordita laid her cheek against the white horse's glossy neck, and murmured:

"Sleep tight tonight, beautiful white one! One night in the stable, and the king's son will make me his bride!"

And again a shower of gems fell sparkling from her lips.

Then Cordita shared her crust of bread with the white horse and the golden bird, took her lantern from the nail, climbed up to her bed among the straw in the loft, and quickly went to sleep. And the king's son snuck out of the stable, fetched the golden dress, climbed quietly up to the loft, and spread the golden dress on the straw beside the sleeping Cordita. For he had found wisdom in silence and now he knew who should be his true bride.

And at sunrise next morning, when Cordita woke up, she found the golden dress gleaming on the straw beside her. So she got up, drew water from the well to wash herself, and put on the golden dress. And when she came out of the stable in the golden dress, her feet still bare and summer's golden bird flying free about her head, the king's son was waiting under the blossoming lime tree. Without a word he took her hand and led her into the house.

Now for once the stepmother and Kapala had also risen at sunrise, for the stepmother hoped that this morning the king's son would give Kapala the golden dress and ride away with her to the royal palace to make her his bride. But when they heard the door open, and found Cordita standing shyly there, wearing the golden dress, her hand in the hand of the king's son, and summer's golden bird flying about her head, they knew that the prince had found his true bride in spite of all their plans. They couldn't say anything because they felt so guilty and ashamed.

Then the king's son said, still holding onto Cordita's hand:

"I have found the maiden which my godmothers promised me. Cordita, will you come home with me to my father's palace and be my bride?"

And Cordita answered softly:

"I will do that gladly."

Kapala gave Cordita the golden shoes and the golden comb, and the stepmother opened the iron chest for her to take the gems; and they both begged her to forgive them.

And Cordita answered gently:

"I will do that gladly. The golden shoes and the golden comb I will take, because they are gifts for a bride but you should keep the gems so that you may both live long and happy lives."

When Cordita put on the golden shoes and combed her hair with the golden comb, she looked every inch a princess. And together they walked hand-in-hand across the flowering courtyard amid the birdsong to the stable where the king's son lifted Cordita on to the white horse in front of him, and held her safely there. Then they set out together on their journey over the snowy mountain.

And summer's golden bird flew with them, so that all along their path the snow melted, and the harsh wind grew soft and warm, and flowers sprang up, and bare bushes burst into green leaf, and on their branches birds began to sing. And every time Cordita spoke, a shower of gems fell from her lips to sparkle among the flowers.

And when they reached the royal palace, the king welcomed Cordita as a much-loved daughter. A great banquet was prepared to celebrate when the prince made her his bride and they lived together in great loving kindness.

When the king grew old and died, the prince and Cordita ruled the kingdom together in gentleness and joy; and wherever Cordita went, the golden bird flew about her head, so that summer always went with her; and there was no poverty anywhere in the kingdom because of the shower of gems which fell from her lips each time she spoke. And all the people loved their beautiful queen; and she was known throughout the land as kind Cordita.

The Poem of Kind Cordita

Early the next morning Sylvia woke up to the sound of distant bells ringing "Christ-mass! Christ-mass! Christ-mass!"

She jumped up in bed; and first she explored the treasures in her stocking – fruit, nuts, chocolate, toys, new gleaming shillings, and, hiding away in the toe, a shy little white sugar mouse.

And as she turned to put her treasures on the table at her bedside, she saw that the Wonder Book lay open at a new page.

Last night Sylvia had wanted to ask the rhyme-elves to paint her a poem about Cordita but she had felt shy, because it was Christmas Eve, and it was a little like asking them for a

Christmas gift. So she had gone to sleep without putting out her Wonder Book or saying her poetry spell. But they must have come even without being called, and they must have charmed the Wonder Book out from under her pillow while she slept; for there, on a new page, was their Christmas gift. The page had a picture of the three little men imprisoned in the block of ice, with the kind Cordita kindling a fire to release them.

When Sylvia had gathered all her treasures in her arms, as well as her present for her mother, and her Wonder Book too, she tiptoed to her mother's door. She stood outside and sang a carol very quietly and then called out very loudly:

"Happy Christmas, Mother!"

Then she went in, gave her mother a special Christmas hug and the picture she had painted for her, and climbed into bed beside her.

When they had looked at Sylvia's picture of the first Christmas together, and her mother had thanked her for it, Sylvia showed her mother all her treasures; and then she opened the Wonder Book, and exclaimed:

"Mother, what do you think? I didn't ask the rhyme-elves for a poem last night but still look – they've written me one anyway!"

Then Sylvia's mother said a very funny thing. She said:

"What do I think, Sylvia? I think you must have a tooth loose!"

Sylvia opened her mouth wide and tapped all along her teeth (both rows); and she found that there actually was one, in the middle at the top, that was a little bit shaky!

And she gasped with surprise:

"I have! Look! How did you guess?"

Her mother explained:

"I guessed because when the rhyme-elves start writing poems without being asked, there usually is a tooth nearly ready to come out."

117

And Sylvia asked:

"Mother, what happens when the tooth does come out?"

And her mother answered:

"Then Elf Prince Frey gives you three wonderful gifts and then you can go to school!"

Sylvia bounced up and down on the bed with excitement, and cried:

"There are so many lovely things waiting to happen to children, aren't there? And wasn't it lucky my tooth came loose just in time for Christmas? Mother, will you read me the rhyme-elves' Christmas present, please!"

And this was Sylvia's Christmas gift from the rhyme-elves, which her mother read to her:

> So kind was Cordita,
> Her heart could kindle fire in snow,
> And cause the iron ice to flow,
> And set cold winter's night aglow.
>
> So kind was Cordita,
> She shared her only crust of bread,
> That hungry fairies might be fed
> And with her love be comforted.
>
> So kind was Cordita,
> About her head flew summer's bird;
> And from her lips with every word
> Fell gems, rejoicing all who heard.
>
> So kind was Cordita,
> A king's son wooed her for his bride,
> And they ruled gently side by side,
> And scattered gladness far and wide.
> So *blessed* was Cordita.

Christmas Day

After breakfast Blackbird came *clip-clop-clopping* along the woodland path. She and the old woodsman were spending Christmas Day with Sylvia and her mother. When the old woodsman came into the white cottage, in his Sunday suit and tall starched collar and stiff hat, he didn't look like his lovely, shabby self but Sylvia didn't mind. She loved him just as much whatever he looked like. She came rushing out of the door to meet him and hug his knees and wish him a happy Christmas.

He tossed her up in his arms and kissed her on the cheek under the mistletoe and gave her a parcel wrapped in scarlet tissue paper. Inside Sylvia found a most beautiful snow bird, which the old woodsman had made from tiny, soft white feathers which wild birds had dropped in the dark wood.

Sylvia cried in delight:

"Oh, Mr Woodsman, how beautiful. I've never seen a bird like this before!"

And the old woodsman answered in his slow, cosy voice:

"I only saw one once myself. It came to take me to the palace of Elf Prince Frey when my first tooth came out."

Then Sylvia asked, excited:

"Will one come for me? I've got a loose tooth – look!"

And the old woodsman bent down and looked at it solemnly, and said:

"Yes, Sylvia, it looks as if that snow bird will be coming for you very soon!"

Then Sylvia gave him the present she'd made, which was a thick round mat of coloured wool for his reading lamp to stand on, and the old woodsman admired it tremendously. And then Blackbird and the old woodsman took Sylvia *clip – clop – clop* to the village, so she could give her Christmas gifts to Joan and Terry and Rosaleen and Margaret and Stephen and Luke, and so that she could get her gifts from them. She also wanted to wish all their mothers a happy Christmas, and to invite all her little friends to her birthday party on the last day of the year.

When they returned to the little white cottage, Sylvia opened all the gifts her friends had given her and played with them. Then they ate Christmas dinner, with the old woodsman enjoying two helpings of the Christmas pudding Sylvia had helped to make, and afterwards the old woodsman put on one of Sylvia's mother's aprons, and he and Sylvia washed up together. At first she grumbled about washing up but he talked to her all the while, noticing something interesting about the shape of every spoon and the flowers painted on every plate and dish, so that it became fun. Sylvia had never realised that washing-up could be so exciting.

When the washing-up was done, all three of them finished decorating the Christmas cake with bleached almonds and glowing red cherries and pale green strips of angelica, ready for tea. And Sylvia said:

"Our Christmas cake looks so lovely. Mother would you mind if I took Sister-in-the-Bushes a slice, to wish her a happy Christmas?"

And her mother replied:

"Of course you may, Sylvia. Although you must remember that Sisters-in-the-Bushes don't really live on our sort of food, you know."

And Sylvia asked:

"What do they live on, Mother?"

And her mother replied:

"They live on love."

Then Sylvia said:

"Oh, I'll take her lots of that as well. But I wish I knew what to give her for a Christmas present."

And her mother answered:

"I think I know what she would like – to see your Christmas tree."

Then Sylvia asked:

"What will I say if she wants to give me a present, Mother?"

And her mother replied:

"Ask her for a story. Sisters-in-the-Bushes live with the gnomes, and the gnomes know the loveliest and the truest stories in the world."

Then the old woodsman helped Sylvia to cut a big slice of the Christmas cake, and Sylvia ran out into the garden with it. She stood by the bushes and called to Sister-in-the-Bushes. She came out and they kissed each other and wished each other a happy Christmas then Sylvia gave Sister-in-the-Bushes the slice of Christmas cake.

And Sister-in-the-Bushes cried:

"How full of good things it is, Sylvia! I just know that the garden birds would love to eat it as a Christmas feast!"

Sylvia thought that would be a wonderful idea:

"Let's give it to them together!"

So they broke the slice of cake into tiny pieces and held them out on their palms. Sister-in-the-Bushes made soft sounds which the birds seemed to understand and they flew towards them from all parts of the garden. They even flew from the dark wood beyond the nut hedge and perched on the children's heads and shoulders.

When the last crumb was finished, the birds sung little winter songs as they spread their wings and flew away. Sister-in-the-Bushes said that they were saying:

"Thank you for our Christmas feast, and a happy Christmas, Sylvia!"

Then Sylvia asked Sister-in-the-Bushes:

"Will you come into our white cottage, and see my Christmas tree, and help me light the candles? I know you don't like houses, but please come in just this once!"

And Sylvia took her hand, and led her through the garden, in through the cottage door and into the dusky living room. Then she lit two tapers from the log fire, and gave one to Sister-in-the-Bushes. Together they went to the tree and very carefully lit each of the thirty-three candles.

Then they sat down on the rug in front of the blazing fire. Sister-in-the-Bushes couldn't stop staring in wonder at the softly shining tree, with its stars and its roses and its candles and its tinsel and its golden baskets and its rosy apples and piled up beneath its branches all the presents for Sylvia's birthday party in their coloured wrapping. And she sighed:

"Oh, Sylvia, you couldn't have given me a lovelier Christmas gift! I can't think of any gift that I could give you which would be even half as lovely as seeing your beautiful Christmas tree!"

Sylvia answered quickly:

"Oh, but Mother says there is. She says you know the loveliest and the truest stories in the world. Would you tell me one of them, please?"

So while they sat together in the firelight, with Sister-in-the-Bushes staring at the beautiful candle-lit tree which shone softly on them from its corner, she told Sylvia the story of the apple tree that bore a star:

The Story of the Apple Tree that Bore a Star

Long, long, long ago, Father Adam and Mother Eva lived in a green garden on the top of the highest mountain in the world. In the green garden the flowers never died, and the trees bore fruit every day of the year. The birds sang wonderful songs in human voices, and all the animals were good except one, and even lions and tigers were as gentle and friendly as lambs.

Father Adam and Mother Eva could eat as much fruit as they wanted from all of the trees except one. This was the most beautiful tree of all, with a trunk of clear crystal, leaves of shining silver, and apples of pure gold.

The one animal in the green garden who was not good was a flame-coloured serpent. He did not really belong there. And one day he came to Mother Eva and said:

"Look at those golden apples, Eva. Aren't they the most beautiful fruits in the whole green garden?"

And Mother Eva looked and said they were.

Then the serpent said again:

"No fruit in the whole green garden tastes as sweet as they do. No fruit in the whole green garden is so juicy and refreshing. Why don't you eat one of these golden apples, Eva?"

And Mother Eva answered:

"Father Adam and I may eat all the other fruits in the green garden; but we may not eat these."

And the serpent asked:

"But would you not like to eat one of these golden apples, Eva?"

And Mother Eva looked longingly at the golden apples and said she would.

Then the serpent began to sing:

"Take and eat, Eva! Eva, take and eat!"

And he wove a spell round Mother Eva with his long, flaming body.

His enchantments worked on Mother Eva, and she stretched out her hand and picked one of the golden apples; and it lay ripe and warm and glowing in her palm.

And she went to Father Adam, and she said:

"Look, Adam – a golden apple from the tree with the trunk of clear crystal and the leaves of shining silver! I'm going to eat it. Eat it with me!"

Now Father Adam wouldn't have taken a golden apple from the tree himself. But when he saw one lying ripe and warm and glowing in Mother Eva's hand he was tempted. Then he saw her bite into it and sigh happily at how delicious it tasted, so when she held it out for him to taste, Father Adam bit into the golden apple, too.

As soon as he bit into the apple, everything went dark. When the darkness lifted, they found they were outside the door of the green garden, on the bare mountainside, and a Shining One was guarding the door with a great sword of fire.

Father Adam stood there with a heavy heart, and stared sadly back at the green garden. And Mother Eva stood too, crying, with the half-eaten golden apple in her hand.

And from all around them they heard the sound of weeping, too; because when the golden apple was eaten, the whole Earth felt sorrow. Soil and stone and crystal, and root and leaf and flower, and river and rain and dewdrop, and air and wind and light and fire, all wept.

For the first time clouds hid the sun and flowers died. Where once there had been warmth and light, now there was cold and darkness. The birds no longer sang in human voices and the good, gentle beasts snarled and killed each other.

And Father Adam said to the Shining One with the sword of fire who guarded the door of the green garden:

"Do we have to stay outside for ever and ever, Shining One? Can we never return to the green garden?"

And the Shining One with the sword of fire replied:

"My sword of fire will never be blown from the door of the green garden until the tree which grows from the core of the golden apple in Eva's hand bears a star for fruit."

So Father Adam and Mother Eva went sadly down the mountainside and in the valley below they found a cave in which to live. Outside the cave Mother Eva planted the core of the golden apple and the next year a tiny tree began to grow from it.

Year after year Father Adam and Mother Eva watched anxiously as the little tree grew larger. Its trunk was not made of clear crystal, like the tree in the green garden, but black and rough to the touch; and its leaves were not leaves of shining silver, but leaves which withered and fell off and left the branches bare.

When the little tree grew big enough to bear fruit, Mother Eva sat beside it night and day to watch it bear a star. But instead it bore an apple, not even a golden apple like the apple the seed had come from, not even an apple like those in the green garden, sweet and juicy and refreshing. This apple was sour, an apple which could go bad.

Hundreds and hundreds of years passed, the trunk grew rougher, and the leaves grew more withered, and the apples grew smaller and harder and greener and sourer, until the time came when anyone who ate them was ill for ever after.

Now in the days before Mother Eva picked the golden apple, if you had looked at the Earth from one of the stars you would have seen that the Earth was a star, too, sending out starlight and singing, as the other stars still do. But after Mother Eva had plucked the apple, the Earth began to lose its light and forget its song. And the sourer the apples grew, the darker and the more silent became the Earth, until the time came when the other stars looked for its light and could see only darkness, and listened for its song and found it no longer made any sound.

And the stars knew that there was only one thing that could help the dark and silent Earth. And that would be the coming of the Christmas Child.

So the Christmas Child began his journey down through the vast golden sky, journeying on his own five-pointed golden star, enclosed in a great five-petalled flower of light shaped like a white wild rose.

As he approached the Earth, he saw that the earthly mother and father to whom he was coming were on a journey, too. And when night came they had nowhere to sleep except a cave; and this was the very same cave that Father Adam and Mother Eva had lived in when they came down the mountainside from the green garden. And outside the cave Mother Eva's sour apple tree was still growing.

At midnight the Christmas Child reached the Earth; and as he entered the cave to be born, he hung his five-pointed golden star, enclosed in its white five-petalled rose of light, on the top branch of the apple tree, where one hard, sour, withered apple was still clinging. And the star, hidden in its flower, sank into the hard, sour, withered apple; and the apple became firm and rosy and sweet and juicy and refreshing. Never again would anyone who ate apples from that tree be ill for ever after.

At the same moment the Earth felt a lessening of the pain which had lasted ever since Mother Eva picked the golden apple. Soil and stone and crystal, and root and leaf and flower, and river and rain and dewdrop, and air and wind and light and fire, all began to rejoice.

And the other stars, as they looked towards the Earth, saw it begin very faintly to shine again. And when they listened hard they could hear it beginning, very softly, to sing its own song again.

And the Shining One who guarded the door of the green garden felt a gentle wind, blowing his fiery sword backward, and he knew that the time had come when the apple tree outside the cave had borne a star for fruit.

And if you cut a thin slice across an apple and hold it to the light, you will see a five-pointed star within a white wild rose in the middle of it. And this can remind you that at the coming of the Christmas Child the pain of the Earth was lightened, and it began to shine and sing again, and the sword of fire was blown aside from the door of the green garden.

The Poem of Eva's Apple

After her story Sister-in-the-Bushes slipped back into the garden, and Sylvia and her mother and the old woodsman had tea and were sitting together round the fire, with the candles on the Advent wreath and on the Christmas tree all lit. Sylvia brought the old woodsman a large, round, rosy apple and said to him:

"Please, Mr Woodsman, will you show me the star and the flower inside the apple?"

And the old woodsman seemed to know all about it because he took out his pocket knife and he cut the apple in half – not down, the way you usually cut an apple, but straight across the core. And already Sylvia could see that when you cut an apple this way the core is the shape of a five-pointed star. Then the old woodsman cut the apple right across again, and gave Sylvia the very thinnest slice you could imagine taken from right across the middle of the apple, with a thin red line of rosy skin encircling it.

And the old woodsman said:

"Now, hold it up to the light!"

And when Sylvia held it up to the Advent candles, it was so thin that the light came shining through, and she saw just what Sister-in-the-Bushes had described; for surrounding the core's five-pointed star there was a white, five-petalled flower the shape of a wild rose, showing very faintly in the apple's creamy flesh.

And Sylvia held it up for her mother to see, and cried:

"Isn't it wonderful, Mother – when you eat an apple, you eat a flower and a star as well!"

And she went to bed that night with her heart still full of this wonder; so that it did not seem at all surprising that when she woke up the next morning the new picture on a new page of her Wonder Book was of Father Adam and Mother Eva and the Shining One with the sword of fire outside the door of the green garden, nor that when she took her Wonder Book into her mother's bed this should be the new poem that her mother read to her:

> Eva plucked the apple,
> And Earth was stricken sore;
> The sword of flame was flickering
> At the green garden's door
> As she came down the mountain,
> Carrying the apple's core.
>
> Eva plucked the apple,
> And Earth's starlight paled;
> Eva plucked the apple,
> And Earth's music failed;
> And soil and stone and crystal
> And rain and river wailed.
>
> Eva's tree bore apples
> Withered, hard and sour,
> Till upon its branches
> At the first Christmas hour
> A golden star descended,
> Enfolded in a flower.

Now Earth's pain is lightened;
The sword's fire backward blows;
Again is heard Earth's music;
Again Earth's starlight glows.
There's a rose within the apple;
There's a star within the rose.

Sylvia's Birthday Poem

Each afternoon on the first five days after Christmas, Sister-in-the-Bushes came into the white cottage at dusk to help Sylvia light the candles on the Christmas tree, and to gaze happily at its beauty while they sat and talked beside the big log fire. And on the fifth afternoon Sylvia said:

"Did you know, Sister-in-the-Bushes, that tomorrow will be the last day of the year?"

And Sister-in-the-Bushes answered, smiling:

"Yes and it will be your birthday, too, won't it, Sylvia?"

Sylvia opened her eyes wide, and asked:

"How did you know?"

And Sister-in-the-Bushes smiled again, and answered:

"I remember you being born. It was seven years ago."

Then Sylvia opened her eyes still wider, and begged:

"Oh, do tell me about when I was born. Did I come down on a golden star in a flower of light, like the Christmas Child?"

And Sister-in-the-Bushes answered:

"You came on a rainbow shell shaped like a crescent moon. It sailed away from the full moon and brought you down to Earth. And tomorrow, when you are seven, a silver bell will ring to call it back, but it will leave you here to go on learning how to live on the Earth."

Sylvia thought about this quietly for a few moments. Then she asked:

"But I did have a star of my own when I was born, didn't I?"

130

And Sister-in-the-Bushes replied:

"Of course you did, Sylvia. It shone high in the sky, right above your white cottage; and it sent down a long, rosy ray of light to warm you; and on the rosy ray your name was written; and that was how your mother knew what name to give you."

And Sylvia asked:

"Will my star do anything new tomorrow, like my moon-boat?"

And Sister-in-the-Bushes replied:

"Indeed it will. It has been waiting for you to be seven so that it can leap the bar of the wide blue air and come closer, to light your earthly way for you and guide you where you ought to go."

Sylvia thought about this quietly, too, for a few moments. Then she asked:

"Did I have any fairy godmothers, like Cordita's prince?"

And Sister-in-the-Bushes answered:

"Yes, Sylvia, you had twelve. And as you lay in your cradle, they all came and stood round it, and blessed you as you lay sleeping; and each of them gave you a gift."

And Sylvia asked:

"And what will they do on my birthday?"

And Sister-in-the-Bushes told her:

"Tonight, when you are in bed, they will stand round you in their magic ring again, and bless you as you lie sleeping again, and bring you fresh fairy graces because you are seven years old."

And Sylvia exclaimed:

"What wonderful things are going to happen tonight, Sister-in-the-Bushes! I think I'll stay awake, so that I can watch my fairy godmothers standing round my bed, and hear the silver bell which will call my moon-boat home, and see my star leap down out of the sky."

But that night when Sylvia went to bed she was so happy and tired that, even though she tried her hardest, she simply couldn't keep awake. And so she did not hear the silver bell call her moon-boat home, nor see her star leap down out of the sky, nor watch her fairy godmothers standing round her bed, after all.

But when she woke up the next morning, there on her bedside table was her mother's birthday gift – a beautiful new Wonder Book all ready for next year, with three hundred and sixty five big empty white pages, and with golden flowers and birds engraved on its blue leather covers. And the old Wonder Book, which had only two or three more pages left for the rhyme-elves to fill, was open at a new page, with a new poem and a picture of Sylvia seven years ago, coming down between the stars on her crescent moon-boat to be born.

And when she had climbed into her mother's bed, and her mother had given her a special birthday kiss, and Sylvia had thanked her for the beautiful new Wonder Book, this was the poem her mother read to her out of the old one:

> Sylvia is seven years old today.
> Seven years ago a rainbow shell
> Left the full moon, to sail away
> And bring her down on Earth to dwell.
> Now she is seven a silver bell
> Calls back her moon-boat to the skies;
> But Sylvia on the Earth must stay,
> And in the ways of Earth grow wise.
> Sylvia is seven years old today.
>
> Sylvia is seven years old today.
> Seven years ago a rosy star,
> Her radiant name written on its ray,
> Warmed her most sweetly from afar.
> Now she is seven it leaps the bar
> Of the blue airy realms, below

To light for her her earthly way
And guide her where she ought to go.
Sylvia is seven years old today.

Sylvia is seven years old today.
Seven years ago twelve fairies stood
Circling the cradle where she lay,
And blessed her sleep, and said she should
Be true and beautiful and good.
Now she is seven their magic ring
Encloses her again, and they
Fresh fairy graces to her bring.
Sylvia is seven years old today.

Sylvia's Birthday

The snow sparkled and the sun shone for Sylvia's birthday. All morning she was happy and busy, helping her mother to prepare for her birthday party; and early in the afternoon Blackbird came *clip-clop-clopping* from the village, with the old woodsman walking beside her in his Sunday suit, and with the log cart piled with children.

There were fir branches spread round Sylvia's place at the table, and under these the old woodsman and Joan and Terry and Rosaleen and Margaret and Stephen and Luke all quietly hid their birthday gifts. Round everybody else's place were holly leaves and berries in shining trails of tinsel, and coloured candles in gilded acorn and beech nut moon and star candle holders, and little bowls of marzipan cherries and strawberries which Sylvia had helped her mother to colour and model. And in the middle of the table stood the big birthday cake, which Sylvia had also helped to make, covered with white icing, with seven coloured candles on the top.

When the lights had been turned off, and Sylvia had lit the seven candles on the cake, and Joan and Terry and Rosaleen and Margaret and Stephen and Luke and the old woodsman and Sylvia's mother had lit the coloured candles round their plates, they all sat down at the table, and watched Sylvia finding their presents among the fir branches. Each time she found one she said "Oh!" with delight, and the children round the table smiled with her happiness.

After tea they lit the candles on the Christmas tree and sang carols; and then they played games – noisy ones and quiet ones, running-about ones and sitting-still ones; and then they asked each other riddles and told each other stories.

Then, because it was New Year's Eve, the old woodsman showed them a game that country children used to play that night when he was a boy. He melted a little lead in an old ladle with a long handle over the log fire, then poured the melted lead into a bowl of cold water. As it cooled it became a new shape, and the old woodsman picked it up and showed it to them and asked:

"What does it look like?"

And all the children shouted together:

"A boat!"

And the old woodsman said:

"That must be the boat that is bringing Peter across the sea."

And he told them about Peter, his little grandson, who was just about their age; and how he had lived in a great city. But Peter was too tall and too thin and too pale and too clever and he wasn't happy in the city and so he and his mother were coming to live in the woods with the old woodsman. The old woodsman hoped that the trees and the flowers and the birds and the animals and Sylvia and the other children would help him to feel better. And tomorrow Blackbird and the old woodsman were meeting Peter's boat and bringing Peter and his mother home.

Sylvia was so excited at the thought of meeting Peter that it seemed like the kind world was giving her an extra birthday gift – a new friend!

Then Joan and Terry and Rosaleen and Margaret and Stephen and Luke took turns to melt a little lead in the ladle with the old woodsman's help; and everyone laughed as they guessed what each shape was and what it meant was going to happen in the New Year. When it came to Sylvia's turn and she held up her odd little lump of lead for everyone to see, everyone shouted, laughing:

"A tooth! Sylvia's is a tooth!"

And the old woodsman added:

"Ah, that's a very special tooth. It means three New Year gifts for Sylvia!"

And Sylvia remembered her mother telling her on Christmas morning that Elf Prince Frey would have three wonderful gifts for her when her first tooth came out; and she felt more excited than ever. And as she tickled her loose tooth with her tongue she was pretty sure that it really was getting shakier.

When the party was finally finished Joan and Terry and Rosaleen and Margaret and Stephen and Luke collected the treasures they had been given from Sylvia's Christmas tree, and said thank you and goodbye. Then the old woodsman packed them all into the log cart; and away went Blackbird, *clip-clop-clopping* back towards the village, taking them all home, tired and happy, to their waiting mothers.

And Sylvia, too, was so tired and happy that she could hardly keep awake long enough to undress and be tucked into bed with all her new birthday toys. But after her mother had tiptoed out of her bedroom and softly closed the door, Sylvia suddenly thought that someone else was in the room. When she turned her sleepy head to look, she saw Sister-in-the-Bushes standing in the moonlight beside her bed.

And Sister-in-the-Bushes bent down and smiled and whispered:

"I've come to bring you your birthday present, Sylvia; but you'll think it a very funny one. Open your mouth!"

And she took Sylvia's hand in hers, and guided it to the shaky tooth, and closed Sylvia's thumb and finger on it; and there was a tiny tug and a tiny pinch, and there lay the tooth in Sylvia's palm!

And Sylvia gulped:

"It does seem like a funny present, Sister-in-the- Bushes!"

And Sister-in-the-Bushes smiled again, and whispered:

"I know; but just put it under your pillow, Sylvia, and see what it will bring you!"

So Sylvia sleepily put the tooth under her pillow and when she looked up again, Sister-in-the-Bushes was gone.

And Sylvia thought dreamily:

"I wonder what it will bring me? It doesn't really matter anyway because now I can go to school!"

And with the tip of her tongue she touched the gap where the tooth had been, and thought how funny it felt, and how lovely it would be to go to school, and how wonderful to have Peter for a friend, and to have Blackbird and the old woodsman to take them both to school each day; and then she didn't think anything more, because the next moment she was sound asleep.

Sylvia and the Three Fairies

Sylvia did not know how long she had been asleep when she heard little sounds of delight, and tiny voices crying:

"Isn't she beautiful? Oh, isn't she beautiful? By sun and moon and stars, how beautiful she is!"

Sylvia opened her eyes; and there, standing all around her bed, watching her with looks and cries of joy, were three fairies.

One was a little knight in shining armour; so Sylvia knew he was an earth fairy. And one had a fish's tail, like a tiny mermaid; so Sylvia knew she was a water fairy. And one had wings; so Sylvia knew she was an air fairy.

And the earth fairy was sheltering his fairy horse under a dandelion plant; and the water fairy was floating in the white blossom of a water lily; and the air fairy was hovering over a purple meadow-plant, landing every now and then on its one of its wing-shaped flowers.

When they saw Sylvia's eyes were open, the earth knight said:

"Beautiful Sylvia, I am Gnome. And how beautiful you are!"

And the water fairy said:

"Beautiful Sylvia, I am Undine. And how beautiful you are!"

And the air fairy said:

"Beautiful Sylvia, I am Sylph. And how beautiful you are!"

And Sylvia said:

"Yes, I remember you all. You showed me how a fairy tree is made. But you couldn't see me then. How is it you can now?"

Then Gnome explained:

"We can see you now because tonight you are seven years old and your first tooth has come out. When little human children lose their first tooth, it is a wonderful moment for fairies!"

And Undine added:

"Yes, we cannot see little children until they are seven and then, in a moment, they suddenly appear and are so very beautiful that we think there is nothing so lovely in the whole wide world!"

And Sylvia asked:

"But how did you know that my tooth came out tonight?"

And Sylph explained:

"Sister-in-the-Bushes told us she had just helped it out, and asked us to come straight to you. She is very anxious you should choose the right tooth-gifts at the palace of Prince Frey but if you give your tooth to Gnome, it will help us to help you to choose the right gifts for you."

Sylvia felt under her pillow, and pulled out her little gleaming tooth, and gave it to Gnome.

And Gnome asked his dandelion:

"Now what shall Sylvia's tooth-gifts be?"

And Undine asked her water lily:

"Now what shall Sylvia's tooth-gifts be?"

And Sylph asked her meadow-plant:

"Now what shall Sylvia's tooth-gifts be?"

Gnome listened for a moment, then said in his hearty, shouting little voice:

"I speak for Earth. Earth's rarest tooth-gift is a winged white horse. It can carry Sylvia to the clouds and back again. Choose this gift, Sylvia."

Undine listened for a moment, then said in her gentle, dreaming voice:

"I speak for Dew. Dew's fairest tooth-gift is a fairy fruit tree. Every night it bears a fairy peach and a fairy pear; and if Sylvia eats them they will keep her strong and beautiful. Choose this gift, Sylvia."

Sylph listened for a moment, then said in her delicate singing voice:

"I speak for Wind. Wind's noblest tooth-gift is a golden key. It will unlock the richest treasure chests in Prince Fray's palace, and fill Sylvia's heart with loving understanding. Choose this gift, Sylvia."

Then Gnome and Undine and Sylph said together:

"When the snow bird comes for you, Sylvia, the tooth-gifts will be waiting. But be sure you choose the right ones!"

Then Gnome, with his fairy horse and his yellow dandelion, and Undine, with her white water lily, and Sylph, with her purple meadow-plant, disappeared in the twinkling of an eye.

And in the twinkling of another eye, Sylvia was sound asleep again.

The Poem of the Three Tooth-Gifts

When Sylvia woke up again at the proper time, she immediately remembered Gnome and Undine and Sylph; and she wondered:

"Were they really here? Or did I dream them?"

Then she remembered about her tooth coming out. She could

feel its little gap with the tip of her tongue, so she knew that that had happened, anyway. And she remembered that she had put the tooth under her pillow, and had given it afterwards to Gnome. So she searched under her pillow but it was nowhere to be found.

So next she turned to her bedside table, in case she had put it there. And there she saw her Wonder Book, open at a new page – the second to last page – and on the page was a new poem, and beside the poem there was a new picture. And as soon as Sylvia saw the picture, she knew that Gnome and Undine and Sylph's visit really had happened. The picture showed Sylvia in bed, and Gnome on his fairy horse beside the yellow dandelion, and Undine floating in her white water lily, and Sylph hovering over her purple meadow-plant.

So she jumped out of bed and ran with her Wonder Book to her mother's room. And they wished each other a very happy New Year. Then Sylvia told her mother about her first tooth coming out, and smiled widely so that her mother could see the little gap. And her mother gave her a special hug and a silver sixpence, because her first tooth had come out.

Then Sylvia's mother read the new poem in the Wonder Book and as Sylvia listened she was doubly sure that Gnome and Undine and Sylph really had visited her; and this is what the poem said:

> What shall Sylvia's tooth-gifts be –
> Rare gifts for Sylvia?
> Around her bed came fairies three,
> With Earth's and Wind's and Water's
>   flower;
> And pondered what enchanted power
> Each should choose for Sylvia's dower.
> What shall Sylvia's tooth-gifts be –
> Fair gifts for Sylvia?

Shouted Gnome right heartily:
"This shall Sylvia's tooth-gift be –
Earth's gift for Sylvia:
A winged and magic horse shall she
Have to take her from Earth's plain
To the clouds and back again –
A white mare with a golden mane!
This shall be her dower from me –
Earth's gift for Sylvia."

Undine murmured dreamily:
"This shall Sylvia's tooth-gift be –
Dew's gift for Sylvia.
She shall have a fairy tree
Which every night for her shall bear
A fairy peach and a fairy pear,
To eat to keep her strong and fair.
This shall be her dower from me –
Dew's gift for Sylvia."

Then sang Sylph melodiously:
"This shall Sylvia's tooth-gift be –
Wind's gift for Sylvia:
She shall have a golden key
Which shall unlock each chest and door
Of Elfland's richest treasure store,
And load her heart with loving lore.
This shall be her dower from me –
Wind's gift for Sylvia."

So these shall Sylvia's tooth-gifts be –
Rare gifts for Sylvia.
A wonder-filled New Year starts she
With a white winged horse, and a golden
    key,
And a peach and a pear on a fairy tree,
And a fairy benedicite –
Rare tooth-gifts from the fairies three –
Fair gifts for Sylvia!

Sylvia and Elf Prince Frey

Sylvia's mother had only just finished reading the poem of the three tooth-gifts when, even though it was early in the morning, they heard Blackbird *clip-clop-clopping* along the woodland path. So Sylvia jumped out of her mother's bed, and ran to the window and opened it. She knelt with her breath melting the ice-ferns which the frost fairies had painted on the glass during the night, while she called:

"Happy New Year, Blackbird! Happy New Year, Mr Woodsman!"

The old woodsman was wearing his Sunday suit and his tall starched collar and his stiff hat; and he called back to her:

"Happy New Year to you, too, Sylvia! Blackbird and I are on our way to meet Peter and his mother. First thing tomorrow morning I'll bring him here to meet you!"

And Sylvia breathed whole banks of ice-ferns off the window in her excitement, and leaned right out to show the old woodsman the gap her tooth had left; and he was tremendously impressed. And he said:

"That means you'll be going to the palace of Prince Frey tonight for your tooth-gifts, Sylvia."

And Sylvia asked, a little anxiously:

"You don't think he'll forget to send his snow bird? If he does, I'll never be able to find my way."

And the old woodsman answered comfortingly:

"Oh no, he never forgets."

When Blackbird had gone *clip-clop-clopping* away, Sylvia ran downstairs to her toy cupboard, and brought out the snow bird the old woodsman had given her for Christmas. She carried it with her all day wondering what exciting things would happen when the fairy snow bird came, and at bedtime she took it to bed with her.

With the snow bird tucked up beside her she didn't think anything of the soft and warm and downy thing she felt brushing her cheek after she had gone to sleep that night. But still she opened her eyes and to her surprise there was a beautiful, real, white snow bird nestling on her pillow and brushing her cheek with his wing.

As soon as the snow bird saw Sylvia was awake, he piped:

"Take hold of my golden ribbon, Sylvia! I have come to take you to the palace of Prince Frey!"

And as soon as Sylvia had grasped the end of the golden ribbon that was round the snow bird's throat, she found herself floating in the air and looking down at a shining little garden on her bed.

She felt a pricking in her heels; and when she turned and looked, she saw that each heel had grown a tiny wing. So she half-flew, half-floated, drawn through the air by the snow bird, until they came to a forest. And the snow bird piped:

"That is a magic forest, Sylvia, and there are two ways of reaching it – one across that narrow river of tar, and one across this wide, wide river of starlight. Which way would you like to go?"

And Sylvia looked down at them. The narrow river of tar was thick and sticky, and the wide, wide river of starlight was beautiful and sparkling, so she answered:

"Oh, Snow bird, let's take the wide, wide river of starlight, please!"

And the snow bird piped back:

"I am glad you chose the river of starlight, Sylvia. The river of tar is narrower, but it is harder to cross, because it drags little children's feet down into it, and clogs their wings, so that they cannot fly. And on the other side of the river of tar a wicked hunter lies in wait, and hunts the children who choose that way; and if he hunts them into his iron stove they can only get out if somebody helps them."

So Sylvia and the snow bird flew across the wide, wide river of starlight and came to the magic forest; and as they flew over the tops of the trees, Sylvia heard a voice crying faintly far below:

"Let me out! Let me out!"

And Sylvia pleaded:

"Dear Snow bird, couldn't we stop and see if we can help?"

So the snow bird folded her white wings, and she and Sylvia floated slowly down into the magic forest.

And all the time the voice, very angry and frightened, kept crying:

"Let me out! Let me out!"

Sylvia ran between the trees towards the sound; and there, in a clearing in the forest, she found an iron stove. The angry, frightened voice was coming from inside.

So Sylvia turned and turned the handle, and shook the door and banged the door and pushed the door and leaned on the door; but the door remained closed tight.

Then the voice called to her from inside the iron stove:

"The only way is to *scrape* a way through. You scrape from your side and I'll scrape from mine."

Sylvia scraped until her fingertips were sore; and at last a tiny hole appeared. As soon as it did the door flew open; and out came a little boy. He looked about the same age as Sylvia, but he was taller and thinner and paler, and the tiny wings on his heels were clogged with tar.

And the little boy thanked her, and said:

"The wicked hunter hunted me into this iron stove when I was on the way to the palace of Prince Frey to get my tooth-gifts."

And Sylvia exclaimed:

"That's where we're going – let's go together!"

But when they took the snow bird's golden ribbon in their hands and tried to fly, they found that the little boy's wings were too heavily clogged with tar; so they walked the rest of the way through the magic forest, with the snow bird fluttering ahead to show them the right path.

And at the edge of the magic forest, the most beautiful fairy prince in the whole world, Prince Frey, came to meet them, and welcomed them into a wonderful palace made of snow. He led them from room to room, and every room was decorated with flowers and filled with treasures; and the fairy prince said kindly:

"Come as often as you like to roam through my palace and explore its treasures!"

Then the pale little boy said that he felt thirsty. So Elf Prince Frey brought golden bowls of wine and milk; and he said to the two children:

"Choose whichever you want to drink."

And the pale little boy said at once:

"Milk is only for babies. *I* shall choose wine, like the grown-ups do. *You* choose wine, too, Sylvia!"

And he took a bowl of the wine, and began to drink it.

This made Sylvia feel a little embarrassed because she really liked milk best; and she was just stretching out her hand to take a bowl of the wine when a soft voice whispered in her ear:

"Choose the milk, Sylvia! Wine is only for grown-ups."

And glancing round, Sylvia caught a glimpse of Sister-in-the-Bushes standing beside her, smiling lovingly.

So Sylvia took the milk; and with every sip she could see, in the crystal mirrors on the walls, that she grew more rosy and beautiful. But when she looked at the little boy, she saw that with every sip he took of the wine he grew taller and thinner and paler.

When Sylvia had drunk the last drop of her milk, she saw that a small golden key lay at the bottom of the bowl. And when the pale little boy had drunk the last drop of his wine, he saw at the bottom of *his* bowl a small key made of lead. They had both received the first of their tooth-gifts!

They ran excitedly around the room, opening the big treasure chests, which were arranged along the walls, with their keys. Sylvia's golden key always unlocked chests of gold and pearls and beautiful things and pictures. But the pale little boy's key of lead only unlocked chests of scissors and knives and compasses and things which grown-ups use.

Sylvia found it very strange that the pale little boy was just as delighted with the treasures that his key of lead unlocked as she was with the treasures her golden key unlocked.

And she said to Elf Prince Frey:

"It doesn't seem fair – I have all the nicest things! Couldn't I lend my golden key to the pale little boy?"

And Prince Frey said, smiling kindly:

"You can't lend it to him, Sylvia, because it will only open the treasure chests for you. But what you *can* do is to share your treasures with him."

Then Elf Prince Frey took the two children into his orchard, in which grew every sort of fruit tree in the world.

And he said to them:

"For your second tooth-gift each of you may choose a fruit tree to be your very own."

Then the pale little boy ran to an apple tree loaded with apples, and cried:

"I shall choose this! You choose an apple tree, too, Sylvia!"

Sylvia felt like perhaps she ought to choose an apple tree as well since he said so and she was just going to when a soft voice whispered in her ear:

"Choose the tree Undine promised you, Sylvia."

And glancing round, Sylvia caught a glimpse of Sister-in-

147

the-Bushes standing beside her, smiling lovingly.

So Sylvia chose a tree which bore a fairy peach and a fairy pear. And when she bit into the fairy peach she felt strong; and when she bit the fairy pear the little gap in her teeth stopped bothering her and her fingertips stopped feeling sore from scraping the iron stove. But when the pale little boy bit his apple, he grew thinner and taller and paler.

And Sylvia felt sorry for him, and she said to Elf Prince Frey:

"It doesn't seem fair – I have all the nicest things! Couldn't I lend my fairy tree to the pale little boy?"

And Prince Frey said, smiling kindly:

"You can't lend it to him, Sylvia, because it will only bear its fairy fruit for you. But what you *can* do is to share its fruit with him."

Then Elf Prince Frey took the two children into his meadow, where many horses were feeding.

And he said to them:

"For your third tooth-gift you may each choose a horse for your very own."

And the two children ran to and fro in great excitement, looking at all the horses and wondering which to choose. And they saw that some horses were very clever, and could count and nod their heads in answer to questions; but that some horses stood quite still and fed quietly, except that every now and again one would strike the ground with his hoof, and then a spring of clear, sweet water would come bubbling out.

Then the pale little boy went up to a clever horse, and put his hand on it, and cried:

"I choose this one! You choose a clever one, too, Sylvia! Just think how wonderful it will be to have a clever horse who can count and answer questions!"

This made Sylvia think that that *would* be quite special; and she was just about to lay her hand on a clever horse, too, when a soft voice whispered in her ear:

"Choose the horse Gnome promised you, Sylvia."

And glancing round, Sylvia caught a glimpse of Sister-in-the-Bushes standing beside her, smiling lovingly.

So Sylvia looked at all the quiet horses, but none of them had wings. But just then one white one lifted its head and looked at her; and Sylvia fell in love with it at once, and went to it and laid her hand upon its back.

Suddenly she felt herself rising, rising, rising in the air, riding the white horse; and her hair was growing longer and streaming out behind her; and the mane of the horse was growing longer, too, and streaming out behind. The horse's long mane and her long hair mingled, and together they turned into wings.

Riding so high above the world on her winged white horse was the most wonderful thing that Sylvia has ever done. As she leaned over his neck and looked down, she saw the strong, kind Earth patiently carrying men and women and children and animals, and stones valiantly helping the Earth to bear their weight. And though it was mid-winter, in the kingdom of Prince Frey she could see all the seasons working – the spring saps rising in the plants to greet the moon; and the warm sunbeams drawing up the tall green cornstalks; and the winds and the bees and the butterflies carrying pollen from flower to flower; and bees making honey.

And in the cornfields she saw birds and animals and earthworms all helping the wheat to grow, and fairies kneading dew and rain and starlight into grain. And everywhere that Prince Frey went, the corn sprang up to meet his smile, and tiny loaves clustered at the top of each corn stalk till it looked like a fairy tree bearing a harvest of fairy bread.

And Sylvia was filled with gratefulness to the Earth and stone and sun and moon and wind and bee and butterfly and bird and beast and worm and flower and fairy and Elf Prince Frey himself.

And there below, Sylvia could also see the pale little boy watching his horse count, quite happy with his choice. But Sylvia was sad for him, because although that might be clever, he was missing all the wonders that could only be seen from high above the world.

And she called down to Elf Prince Frey:

"It doesn't seem fair – I have all the nicest things! Couldn't I lend my winged horse to the pale little boy?"

And Prince Frey smiled up at her, and said kindly:

"You can't lend it to him, Sylvia, because it will only soar to the clouds for you. But what you *can* do is to take him up with you sometimes."

And then a trumpet sounded; and the winged horse carried Sylvia swiftly away; and soon she could see the little shining garden below her on her bed. And the horse sank slowly down; and the wings turned back into mane and hair; and before Sylvia knew it, she was back inside the little garden and was thinking drowsily:

"That trumpet is Mother's cockerel crowing!"

And then she was fast asleep.

The Poem of the Fairy Bread

When Sylvia woke up, she again felt something soft and warm and downy brushing her cheek; and when she turned her head, there was a beautiful white snow bird nestling on her pillow once again. At first she thought she must be having the same dream over again, until she realised that there was no golden ribbon around this snow bird's throat. It wasn't Elf Prince Frey's snow bird this time. It was the snow bird which the old woodsman had made for her from feathers from the wood.

And when she turned to look at her Wonder Book, she saw another snow bird. The Wonder Book was open at a new page, and on the page was a new poem, and beside the poem was a picture of her and the little boy she had rescued from the iron stove being guided through the magic forest by the snow bird of Prince Frey. And when she picked up the Wonder Book to look at the picture more closely, she saw that this page was the very last page of all.

So when she took the book into her mother's bed, she said:

"Mother, I feel rather sad. This is the rhyme-elves' last poem in this Wonder Book. But they will go on painting poems in my new one, won't they?"

And her mother answered:

"Yes, if you go on being grateful to them, Sylvia. And now that you have a winged white horse, they'll help you to bring back your own poems from the clouds, as well."

Then they looked back through the full Wonder Book together – laughing at Lordly Cockerel and Hugin's turnip, and remembering with joy the youngest prince, and the star princess Helia, and kind Cordita, and Knight Michael.

And then Sylvia's mother read the last poem in the Wonder Book; and this was it:

Thank you, Earth beneath my feet;
Thank you, stones that keep Earth firm;
Flowers, that work to make food sweet;
Every bird and beast and worm
Which helps the soil bring forth the wheat;
And fairies, kneading dew and rain
And starlight into glowing grain.
Fairy trees bear fairy bread,
That elves and children may be fed.

Thank you, Sun, that from the skies
Makes the tall green corn stalks grow;
Winds and bees and butterflies,
Ferrying pollen to and fro;
Moon, that makes the spring saps rise;
Frey, whose warming smile can cause
Golden loaves to spring from straws.
Fairy trees bear fairy bread,
That elves and children may be fed.

Sylvia and Peter

Sylvia was getting dressed after listening to the poem of the fairy bread when she heard Blackbird *clip-clop-clopping* along the woodland path. She had just enough time to comb out the tangles in her curls, and to put on the proper velvet hair ribbon from the box St Nicholas had given her, before she heard the old woodsman's slow, crunching step on the snow. She climbed up on to the window seat to open her bedroom window; and the old woodsman turned up his kind, wise old face, and called:

"Good morning, Sylvia! I've brought you Peter!"

And when Sylvia looked at the little boy beside him, the little grandson who was too pale and too tall and too thin and too clever, she cried "Oh!" Who do you think it was but the pale little boy she had been with all night in the kingdom of Prince Frey!

And when Peter looked up and saw Sylvia, he cried "Oh!" too. And they smiled at each other; and already they felt like friends.

And as Sylvia jumped down from the window seat, her feet went hop-skip-and-jump, and she was so bubbling with happiness that she sang a little song:

"Oh, how lovely it is to be seven years old,
and to have given your first tooth to the
fairies!
Oh, how lovely it is to be starting school
next week!
Oh, how lovely it is to have Prince Frey for
your friend, and his palace to roam in!
Oh, how lovely it is to have a winged white
horse and a golden key and a fairy fruit
tree and a Peter to share them with!
What a beautiful new New Year!"

And Sylvia ran downstairs to join Peter, smiling brightly.

Goodbye, Sylvia – just for now.

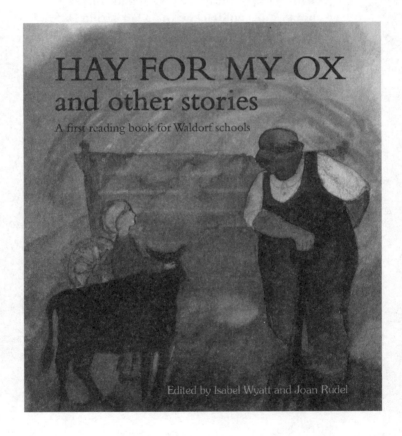

THE EIGHT-YEAR-OLD
LEGEND BOOK

Isabel Wyatt

www.florisbooks.co.uk

KING
BEETLE-TAMER

Isabel Wyatt

www.florisbooks.co.uk

THE BOOK OF
FAIRY PRINCES

Isabel Wyatt

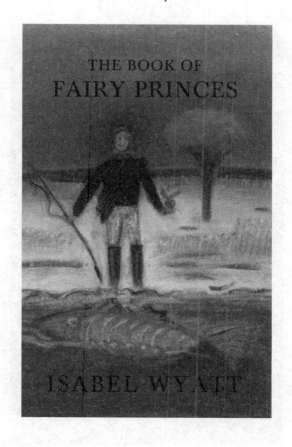

www.florisbooks.co.uk

NORSE
HERO TALES

Isabel Wyatt

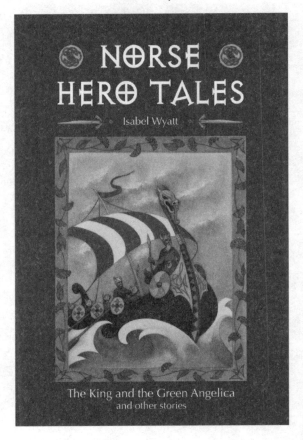

www.florisbooks.co.uk

Legends of
King Arthur

Isabel Wyatt

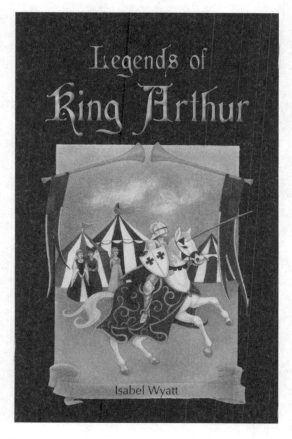

www.florisbooks.co.uk